SOMEBODY UP THERE HATES YOU

SOMEBODY UP THERE HATES YOU

Hollis Seamon

ALGONQUIN   2013

Published by

Algonquin Young Readers

An imprint of Algonquin Books of Chapel Hill

P.O. Box 2225

Chapel Hill, NC 27514

a division of

Workman Publishing

225 Varick Street

New York, New York 10014

LIBRARY OF CONGRESS CATALOGING-IN-PUBLICATION DATA

Seamon, Hollis.

Somebody up there hates you : a novel/Hollis Seamon.—First edition.

pages cm

Summary: Dying of cancer in a hospice, seventeen-year-old prankster
Richard has big plans for his final days.

ISBN 978-1-61620-260-6

[1. Terminally ill—Fiction.   2. Hospices (Terminal care)—Fiction.]   I. Title.

PZ7.S43924So 2013

[Fic]—dc23   2013008476

10 9 8 7 6 5 4 3 2 1

First Edition

For all the kids I came to know at Babies Hospital,
Columbia-Presbyterian Medical Center, 1976–1990. Your
faces fill my dreams and your voices still echo in my ears.

Wait for death with a cheerful mind.

Marcus Aurelius, *Meditations*

SOMEBODY UP THERE HATES YOU

Part I

OCTOBER 30 – NOVEMBER 1

I SHIT YOU NOT. Hey, I'm totally reliable, sweartogod. I, Richard Casey—aka the Incredible Dying Boy—actually do live, temporarily, in the very hospice unit I'm going to tell you about. Third floor, Hilltop Hospital, in the city of Hudson, the great state of New York.

Let me tell you just one thing about this particular hospice. Picture this: right in front of the elevator that spits people into our little hospice home, there is a *harpist*. No joke. Right there in our lobby, every damn day, this old lady with white hair and weird long skirts sits by a honking huge harp and strums her heart out. Or plucks, whatever. The harp makes all these sappy sweet notes that stick in your throat.

How weird is that? I mean, isn't that, like, a bit premature? Hey, we're not dead yet. But it's pretty amusing at times, in its own strange way, this whole harp thing. I can sit there in my wheelchair, on a good day, and watch people get off that elevator. They're here to visit their dying somebody and they walk right into our little lobby and that music hits them and they sort of stumble and wobble, go pale. They have got to be thinking, just for a second, that they've skipped right over the whole death and funeral mess and gone straight to heaven. Most of them back up at least three steps, and some of them actually press the elevator button or claw at its closed doors, trying to escape. It's easy to read their minds: *they're* not the ones dying, right? So why are *they* here? How did *they* end up in harp-land? It freaks them right out, and I just have to laugh. The nurses tell me that harp music is soothing and spiritual and good for the patients. Okay, I say, fine. Maybe for the 95 percent of the patients who are ancient, like sixty and above, it's good. But what about for me? Or Sylvie? Me and Sylvie, I say, we're *kids*. We're *teenagers* and we're dying, too, and what about *our* rights?

Okay, that's kind of harsh, I admit. Because the nurses really are sort of cool and they get all teary when I say that, because no one, and I mean no one, wants to think about kids dying. But we are, so I say, *Deal with it.* Everybody dies, dudes and dudettes. That's the name of the game.

But that's not what I want to talk about, really. Dying is pretty boring, if you get right down to it. It's the living here that's actually interesting, a whole lot more than I ever would have imagined when I first got tossed in here, kicking and cursing.

Anyway, there is some mad stuff that goes on. Like what me and Sylvie did, night before Halloween, right in front of that elevator. It was classic.

Okay, so maybe I better explain. My grandma—who isn't as old as you'd think, because the women in my family have babies real young, by mistake mostly—once told me that in New Jersey, when she was a kid, there was this amazing night-before-Halloween thing that they called Cabbage Night. On this night, parents actually *sent* their kids out into the night to go crazy. Grandma says that there was only one Cabbage Night rule in her house: be home by midnight. Even on a school night! I mean, you can do a whole lot of very bad and very funny stuff between sunset—let's say around six—and midnight, right? Here's Grandma's list of stuff they'd do: run through people's yards and leap over their fences, screaming like banshees; throw eggs at everything and everybody in sight; put dog poop in paper bags, light the bags on fire and throw them on someone's front porch, then watch the homeowner, usually the dad if there's one around, stamp out the fires

5

and spray himself knee-deep in shit; hit kids with sacks of flour until everybody is white as ghosts; steal anything that strikes your fancy and isn't nailed down; tip over gravestones; tie nerdy kids to gravestones and leave them there until about 11:58; break empty beer bottles— after you drink the beer somebody's cool uncle bought you—on curbs and threaten to cut other kids' throats; set out nails point-up on the streets, hoping to pierce car tires; and—well, whatever kids could think of. I mean, it's just so unbelievable to me that the parents *let* this stuff go on, year after year. Grandma says that when she was a kid, she came home at midnight every year bruised, covered in yolk, flour and beer, half-drunk and all the way exhausted. And here's the best thing: no one *cared*. In fact, her parents hadn't even bothered to wait up for her. Grandma says her folks figured, what the hey, better the kids get this shit out of their systems once a year than dribble out bits of badness every other day on the calendar. So they just said, "Go ahead on and get it over with. Just don't kill anybody, okay?"

I swear, this is all relevant to me and Sylvie's own little Cabbage Night performance because, as I believe I mentioned, we're *kids,* hospice hostages or not.

Luckily, that was one of the days that Sylvie was feeling strong enough to get up. Or she *made* herself strong enough, because I'd been bugging her for three days, telling her how funny this whole thing was going to be. Anyway, we waited until 5:30 P.M., October 30. The harp lady knocks off, unless someone requests her services, at 5:00 P.M. And 5:30 is when most of the long-faced loved ones show up to visit. And the nurses are real busy with supper trays and whatnot. So here's what we did.

We donned our preplanned, not-so-gay attire in our separate rooms, and then we wheeled ourselves quietly into the little lobby and we took up the harpy's usual space. We sat in our wheelchairs with, like, insane death mask makeup on our faces—pale green with big black circles around our eyes and streaks of red dripping from our lips. (One of Sylvie's little brothers brought her a vampire makeup kit and had the sense to keep his trap shut about it. Good kid.) And we had my collector's item Black Sabbath T-shirts on, and Sylvie—it surprised me that she had the energy, but the girl was really into it, I guess—she had made a big red devil fork thing out of an IV pole. She'd actually painted the whole thing with nail polish, a real project, and she was holding on to that. And I'd put one of my uncle's rave tapes—all screaming cool distortion—into the CD player on my lap, and we blasted that sucker every time some poor fool stepped off the elevator. And I held up my sign—GOING DOWN—THIS MEANS

YOU!!!!!—written in fake flames. Whenever somebody gasped and backed up, me and Sylvie, we cackled and screeched like insane demons.

Okay, so it was just a childish joke. Funny as all hell, though. But Sylvie—that girl is much tougher than you'd think, given she's about five feet nothing and bald—she took it maybe a smidge too far. See, she'd planned something she didn't tell me about, something totally in the Cabbage Night tradition that she'd come up with on her own and kept quiet about. And she pulled it off without blinking an eye.

Here's what Sylvie did: she reached behind her back and pulled out a cigarette lighter and three boxes of Kleenex. She was quick as anything. She clicked the lighter and lit those babies up—one, two, three—and threw them down on the floor. No shit! Real flames, shooting all over the place. For about one millisecond. Then all hell really did break loose. Nurses and doctors and custodians and volunteers and counselors and food service dudes and probably the priests and rabbis, too—there are always about six guys in black wandering our little hallway—they all came running and shouting, and about nine thousand feet stomped out those three little fires.

And me and Sylvie, we howled. We laughed our asses off, nearly fell out of our chairs. We just could not stop, even when everyone started yelling at us and telling us to go back to our rooms and not come out again. Because that was even funnier—them sending us to our rooms like little kids. Some punishment. I mean, what were they going to do, kill us? Sentence us to death?

But, really, the best part for me was when one of the visitors, Mrs. Elkins's son—I know him, I played gin rummy with him in the visitors' lounge once—grabbed me by the arm and screamed in my face: "What's the *matter* with you, Richie? Where's your respect? What the hell is the *matter* with you?"

And I got to say one of my favorite lines, the one I pull out umpteen times a day, whenever some new priest or therapist or rabbi or nurse or intern or floor-washer or visitor or whoever asks me what's wrong with me. They can't ever seem to quite get it. Obviously, I'm way too young to be here, so what's the story? Here's how these conversations always play out: They go, "Why are you here? What's wrong with you, son?" And I go—straight face, big innocent eyes—"I have SUTHY Syndrome." And when they go all blank and say, essentially, "Huh?" I get to say it again. "SUTHY Syndrome. It's an acronym." Some of them don't even know what that means, but I always wait a beat and then spell it out: "I've got Somebody Up There Hates You Syndrome."

You know, it's really a pretty good diagnosis, don't you think? For me, for Sylvie, for anybody our age who ends up here and places like it, usually after what our obits will soon call a "courageous battle with fill-in-the-blank."

How else you going to account for us? SUTHY is the only answer that makes any damn sense.

***

Anyway, that was the last time I saw Sylvie come out of her room for a couple days. I think it took a lot out of her, all that preparation and excitement. I mean, I can't pretend to know the girl all that well since we just met when we both ended up here. I got here first, and she showed up a day or so later, and we met in the hall and both asked, exactly the same minute, sweartogod, what all of us long-term hospital brats ask one another: "What you in for, man?" And she said—because, like I said, she's tougher than me, really, and never beats around bushes—"I'm here because the shitheads think I'm dying. But I'm not." And I said, because I get, like, tongue-tied sometimes around girls, especially cool ones like Sylvie, I said, "Yeah, me too." But I didn't know which part I was "me too-ing"—the dying or the not. It's sometimes not so clear-cut as you'd think, despite the term *terminal*. I mean, who can really say?

Anyway, at least Sylvie got to get in trouble on Cabbage

Night, like any un-SUTHY-stricken kid. When her family arrived on the scene, her father bawled her out for, like, an hour; I heard him. Then he lashed into the little bro who'd supplied the makeup, and the kid ran out of Sylvie's room like a scared rabbit. That man has one mad-ass temper. Sylvie's mother yelled at her, too, and then sat in the hall and cried.

But let me say this right now: it was *so* worth it. Those flames, for just a second, they were real. Hot and bright and totally real, and for a few minutes afterward you could smell smoke instead of stale hospital air. Real smoke. And, hey, Sylvie got to wear makeup, and that was a real plus. I know she liked the makeup. She's a girl, you know, even if she looks like some Halloween joke now all the time. At least I can still see her, the real girl under the death mask.

So here's what happened next. After the whole Cabbage Night performance, I was beat. And being beat at this point in my life is like nothing you've ever experienced, I assure you. Let's face it, I'm in pretty poor shape. I mean, I don't want to dwell on disease details and all that, because it's so boring and disgusting, but things get a tad rough, especially in the evening. And that's an ordinary evening—this was Cabbage Night! I wish I could say I stayed up until midnight, like Grandma used to, but not so. I rolled myself into my room at, like, seven thirty, and then I sat in my chair, shaking and trying not to throw up, for about twenty-five minutes before Jeannette, who's one of my favorite nurses, black woman with an easy smile, she came in and said, "Well, well, Mr. Devil-Man, you're not looking so energetic now. You need some help in here?"

And I tried to smile. But my face was stiff with makeup gunk and my guts were heaving. Luckily, I don't eat anymore—my choice. Simple common sense decision for those in our position: if you don't eat, you don't have to shit. If you've ever sat on a pink plastic bedpan while people hover around your bed, patting your back and holding you up by the armpits, and there you are, trapped, and your guts are running like crazy, you get it. In hospice, they don't force you to eat or even drink Boost. It's cool with them if you choose to go just a tad more gentle into that good night. Anyway, before you could say "Boo," Jeannette had a nice warm washcloth and she was wiping my face. And chuckling to herself the whole time. Dipping the formerly white washcloth into a basin of water that was swirling green, black and red and laughing, shaking her head. When she was done, she grabbed me under the arms and hoisted me up onto my mattress like I was three years old. I mean, this woman is strong. I'm skinny, sure, but I've grown a lot in the past year. I'm almost 6'2", rough estimate. That's why I like it that 82 percent of nurses, according to the Richie Casey Unscientific Survey conducted over, like, a million years in and out of an amazing array of hospitals, are overweight. They carry muscle under the blubber and, man, can they lift. That's the kind of thing you come to appreciate when most of your own muscle power has gone with the wind. When you've got legs like toothpicks and a rib cage like a turkey carcass the day after Thanksgiving. Oh, and something like 54 percent of nurses smoke. Of course they know it's a lethal habit, but considering what they see, hear and smell every day, do you blame them? I'd love to smoke, too—and come to think of it, that's something they should also allow us here in hospice, right? I'm going to bring that up with the administrators, I swear. Add it to my list.

Jeannette fussed with the sheets for a minute, then she put her hands on her hips and grinned down at me. "That little drama you created was fun, my man, I'll admit it. You and your girlfriend sure did break up the monotony, and I appreciate that." Then the grin changed to a fierce scowl, scarier than any mask ever invented. Like Jeannette's mouth grew fangs and her eyes spit sparks, sweartogod. "Only, if you two ever light a fire in this place again, you will be one sorry pair. If I catch either of you with a lighter or a match or two sticks you're rubbing together, you will pay, big-time. And I do mean pay. Got it?"

"Yes, ma'am. Got it," I said. But, really, I was so stuck on hearing someone refer to Sylvie as my girlfriend and the two of us as a pair that I kind of lost track of everything else. And then Jeannette slapped a brand-new pain patch on my shoulder. That's Fentanyl, every three days, 50 mg, some good stuff. Not quite as good as Dilaudid, IV, but I'm done with needles. No more pokes, pinches, pricks. That's in the past. And they can still go up on the Fentanyl—will, they told me, whenever I ask. I think those things go up to 100 mg. After that, straight onto morphine, any dose, any time. They promised. Always nice to have a plan for the future.

Jeannette also rubbed the antinausea gel that I call Puke-Away on my wrist, and I was happy as a little clam, drifting to sleep in a world where Sylvie and I went to some chick flick together—some lame romance that she'd talked me into—and that was okay because the next week we'd go to see the new Terminator for me. And then we went and got a pepperoni-sausage-double-cheese pizza, and then we fooled around on the big couch in her basement, and she let me get further than ever before, my hands all over her, everywhere. Lips and tongue, too. I mean, I'd almost reached heaven.

And then a real devil paid me a visit. Sylvie's father. Smelling like Marlboro smoke and bourbon, his face sweaty and purply-red. Porcupine bristles on his cheeks. I mean, the man just walked in. And that's one of the worst things about this place and every other hospital room on earth. *Anyone* can just stroll on in. No one even knocks. There is not one iota of privacy in this place. I mean, sure, there are doors on our rooms and sometimes we can keep them shut for about twelve seconds at a time, but the doors have glass windows in them—as in totally transparent. So there you are, on display, day and night. Enough to make a grown kid cry. And don't even try taping a poster or hanging a towel over those windows. Nothing attracts a legion of irate nurses and antsy therapists more than that.

Here's what I'd like to say about this, to everyone. Listen up: we're teenagers. At home, we'd have KEEP OUT signs on our bedroom doors and—duh!—locks. We would slam our doors in everyone's faces and hang out alone in our bolted, private, sanctuary rooms. Free at last, praise god almighty, free at last.

But here? Hell, no. An example: here, Sylvie's mother and her three little brothers hang around her room all day, every day. Hour by hour, minute by minute, *all day.* The little ones, twins I think, run Matchbox cars around the railings of her bed, and the biggest one—the makeup supplier—sits in a corner with a stack of comic books. Her mother clucks around her nonstop, all red-eyed and swollen-faced. Once, I heard Sylvie yelling at her mother, who'd probably just asked her something simple like, "Do you want another pillow, honey?" Sylvie just flat-out screamed, "No, I don't. I want to be left alone. Leave me alooooooooooooooooooooooooone." Sweartogod, that last syllable went on for, like, twenty seconds until Sylvie ran out of breath. Then her mother—short little dark-haired Italian lady, all round and soft—and the three little boys scooted their asses out of there, every one of them in tears. Then I heard Sylvie groaning in her bed, saying, "Shit, shit, shit, shit, shit." And I didn't go anywhere near that room that afternoon. After that, the boys never come in at night anymore and the mother leaves around seven. Now it's Sylvie's father who camps on the fold-out in her room every night. So it's still the no-privacy routine: mother and bros all day, father at night. And when the father is in there, Sylvie never, ever yells at him.

And let me be clear about this: that man scares the bejesus out of me, even when I'm *not* dreaming about his daughter. That man is so mad, so furious, so sad and so, I don't even know how to say it, so, like, *nuclear-blasted* by his daughter's dying that he gives off toxic fumes. No lie, the man glows orange and smells like rotten eggs. Pure sulfur, I swear, running in his veins. And he hates everybody. He's a lawyer, Sylvie says, but I don't know—he seems more like the fucking Godfather to me.

And this is the guy who just stomps on into my room and leans over my bed on Cabbage Night itself. Talk about vicious tricks. I am more than a little stoned and a little horny and beyond exhausted, so all of this has what you might call

17

a nightmare quality about it. Worst case dreamland scenario, come to life. First, the man rattles the metal side of my bed. He leans over and hisses, "You awake, wiseass?"

And I let my eyes open. His bloodshot eyes are about six inches from mine, and he's breathing dragon breath all over my face. I put one hand under the sheet, on the red call button, just in case. Here's the thing: you're helpless in one of these beds. It's a goddamn *crib*. Like you're a *baby*. Talk about sitting ducks. So your only means of help is the call button. "Yes, sir," I say. "I'm awake."

He leans in even closer and he says, "Then listen up, asshole. You stay away from Sylvia. Leave her the hell alone." His eyes go all watery and he says, "Do you know how tired out she is after your little prank? She collapsed in her room, and the nurse could hardly get a blood pressure. It was like—like, nothing. Scared the crap out of me. You little prick." He reaches out a hand and grabs the front of my T-shirt, still the Black Sabbath one. "I don't know what kind of lowlife bitch raised you or why your parents aren't even here, but I'm filling in for them, okay? And if you go near Sylvia again, you'll—"

But he doesn't get to finish, because I sit up, roaring. And I just start screaming and swinging. Because no one, and I mean no one, calls my mom a lowlife bitch. I get in one good fist to his mouth before nineteen people run into the room and pull the man away from my bed. It wasn't much, but I had the satisfaction of seeing blood curling down his lips before Edward, the huge gay nurse, shoves him out of my room, hard. See, Edward doesn't like this man a bit because of an earlier shoving incident at the nurses' station, which I heard all about. Stories like that fly up and down the hallways like demented bats. Any kind of excitement, any slice of good gossip, I mean, that's our daily bread. And that day, the day of the incident, there was yelling and cursing and security called and all kinds of good shit to liven things up. Anyway, let us just say that Edward is not a fan of Sylvie's old man. And that's fine, because you want Edward on your side, trust me, and I'm pretty sure he'll always be on mine. Edward's got my back.

And then Jeannette sits with me for a while, cleaning up my knuckles, which just split wide open on the man's teeth. She wraps gauze around my right hand, sighing and *tsk*ing the whole time, muttering under her breath. I try to explain and only get as far as saying, "He said my mom was—" and she hushes me with a pat on the shoulder.

"I know, honey. You just lie back now and rest. Your heart is going like a hammer. I don't like that. Just shush now."

19

And I fall asleep with her hand soothing my forehead, and it's almost like having my mom with me. Even though I'd been so happy that Mom *wasn't* going to be here for a while, now it seems like I want her. I don't know; it's real complicated, isn't it? Families. Teenagers and parents. It's all very strange.

Here's the thing. It's one of the parts of hospice that drives everybody crazy. Families. In the regular hospital wards, they keep some kind of check on how many family members can show up at one time and bother you, and there are some sort of visiting hours and times when no one's supposed to be there, so you get a little time off. (Except for the Puerto Rican families in the big hospital in New York. Man, no one could keep those people out: grandpas, great-grand-somebodies, seventeen aunts with three kids each, never mind the parents and siblings— everyone came, carrying some kind of food in aluminum containers, smelling like garlic and spice and onion—the whole *familia* showing up day and night. Best damn meals I ever had, whenever my roommate was PR or Dominican or some other kind of Spanish dude. Or, come to think of it, an Orthodox Jew—then all kinds of stuff from the deli showed up. A feast. Here's Richie's free advice to all: if you're going to be in a hospital for a while, claim you need to eat kosher. They can't manage that in the institutional kitchen, so they order out. Brisket, bialys, corned beef on rye, noodle pudding, all of that.)

But here it's a whole different story. No rules about visiting hours and limiting the invaders. Here, as they like to remind everyone, they're "treating the whole family." Great, so it's, like, mad crowded in some rooms, and even at midnight there are people parked all over the place, bored and impatient and stressed and total pains in the ass. Nonstop. Like living in the subway. It stinks.

Okay, back to topic: my mom, the story, short version. Whenever I'm in the hospital, my mom comes in on her lunch hour and late every night and she sleeps in my room on the fold-out or cot or whatever she can round up. I mean, she's kept up this routine, on and off, since I was eleven and started hanging out, way too much, in hospitals. Some of those stays were, like, months and months. Some just days. But she's always been right there, curled up on some lousy cot, all night, every night. She's got to keep working, so she can't hang around with me all day. My mom had me when she was my age exactly—seventeen. And there were only us two, and she worked two jobs—whatever she could get, and luckily she's good with numbers and can keep books and stuff like that, but sometimes it was just cashiering in

Price Chopper. She worked her butt off, always, and she kept us in health insurance totally on her own.

But my mom took a leave of absence from both jobs just recently, when the word *terminal* kept popping up on my charts and when, finally, the word *hospice* became part of my permanent temporary address. My mom, who never even got to sit her butt down and rest on Sunday all of my life, my mom took leave. My mom took what her prick of a boss calls compassionate leave: as in, no paychecks. I mean, how fucking compassionate is that? But she says she doesn't care about that. What matters is that she's been with me day and night now. And I swear she looks sicker than me, and she shakes and cries and has to go out for a smoke every half hour. At night, when she comes back in, I let her kiss me good night like I'm two years old, and then she falls asleep and I look at her curled up on that crappy couch, her cheeks all sunk in and her eyes all puffy, and I think I'm going to lose it. And sometimes I do, the only fucking time the sadness comes through and I want to kill anybody who hurts her and, yes, I'm aware that nobody else on earth could hurt her like I'm doing right now. And that's the worst of all. That's SUTHY with a vengeance. It just sucks, all of it.

***

Deep breath here. Let it go, Richard. Deal. Three more deep breaths. Count backward from one hundred. Ninety-nine. Ninety-eight. Ninety-seven. Ninety-six. Ninety-five. Ninety-four. Ninety-three . . .

Okay. So, this week, I got a reprieve. My mom got the flu. Big-time fevers, hacking cough, the whole bit. Maybe some nasty kind, pending blood tests. And that's one thing even hospice can't allow for its visitors. Flu. Crazy, right? I mean, we're all dying anyway, but they can't be allowed to speed up the process with a friendly push from a rogue virus. Don't even ask. None of it makes any sense, and it makes my head hurt to look for logic.

When I heard that Mom was really sick, at first I was scared. Funnily enough, I was worried about her health—and that's a very strange turnaround, let me tell you. But suddenly, it hit me: I was going to have a week without parental supervision. I was going to enter adolescent nirvana, the week everybody dreams about when they're seventeen, the week the folks leave you home alone. Sure, they call eighteen times a day—but calling ain't seeing, is it? Calling ain't supervising every minute. Calling can't see the beer can pyramid behind you and the half-fried pieces of bacon stuck to the kitchen ceiling where your friends had a weird kind of tossing contest. Calling is just a tiny Band-Aid on teenage wreckage.

So, yeah, Mom's called me constantly this week—and called. And called. And called. And she said that she was getting a little better each day, so I could stop worrying. But I also knew that my time of relative freedom was short.

Naturally, I was going to be as bad as I could, while I could. That was the plan. But we all know what happens to the best-laid—as well as the most half-assed—plans of mice and men, don't we? Absofuckinglutely.

I WAKE UP ON Halloween feeling really down. I had a dream—one where it was Halloween morning, long ago. It was like one of the best days of my life came back, like it had just been tucked away behind my eyelids all this time, waiting for me to relive it. This time of year was always my favorite: the best kid-holiday in the world, followed directly by the buildup to my birthday, November 12—I mean, that is kid heaven. In the dream, things were just like they had been, once upon a time. I was maybe eight years old and totally, insanely excited about my werewolf costume. This was about three years before the real monsters marched into my life. Surgeons, oncologists, radiologists, all those guys with knives and poisons and lethal rays. This was in the good old days, when monsters were fantasy.

Anyway, in this dream, just like in real life, Mom had sewn strands of brown yarn onto a brown turtleneck sweater and brown corduroy pants and even onto a pair of old brown work gloves. Then she taped yarn to a pair of brown boots so I'd be hairy all over. And she'd let me get one of the coolest masks ever—blew a big part of her paycheck at the Halloween store in the mall in Albany. We always made a special October trip up there. That place, it was my idea of paradise. They kept it kind of dark, with blue and green lights flashing around and tapes of screams playing all the time. And it was full of all kinds of masks, all hanging on the walls. I used to believe that the creatures lived inside those walls and just stuck their faces out to let me know they were there. And there were long capes and swords and suits of armor and . . . and everything way too expensive, but Mom always let me buy something incredibly cool, every year. That year, it was the werewolf mask. It had a long rubber snout and an open mouth full of fangs and a red tongue. Spiky wolf-ears and long gray-black fur sticking up on top. I loved it and would barely take it off, even to eat. So there I was, jumping around our little apartment, completely crazed about taking the whole costume to school for the playground parade we'd have in the afternoon. And my mom was laughing at me as she packed the outfit into a plastic bag. "Calm down, kiddo.

You just have to wait a little bit, Rich-Man," she said. And she leaned over and ran a hand over my hair.

And then the dream shifted and it was the parade, and in dreamworld I swear I saw every kid in my third grade class: their faces, their costumes. Every single one, just like they were when we were all eight. Sharp as day, I could see their faces. And I could smell the inside of my mask—sweaty rubber and Snickers from my breath. It was all perfect: we were outside on this clear crisp day, leaves crunchy under our feet. We were allowed to howl and screech, as long as we stayed in line. And I knew, like you do in dreams, just know things, that Sylvie was ahead of me in line, only one person away. Like she'd just showed up for the parade, like she was a new girl in our class. And she turned her head and it was Sylvie like I never saw her, except in some pictures tacked to the bulletin board in her room, maybe: Sylvie with long black hair and sparkling brown eyes and dimples in chubby cheeks. Sylvie in a witch costume, pointy black hat that she'd painted stars and moons on and a long black dress that dragged on the ground. And I could see that she was going to trip on her witch-skirt, so I ran up behind her—oh, man, am I a chivalrous werewolf—and picked up the edge of her skirt and marched behind her, her grinning over her shoulder at me the whole time. And then there was a great big wind, and

27

everything—poof—blew away. And I was left with a tiny scrap of black stuff in my glove and most of the yarn gone from my boots.

I mean, that's enough to break anybody's heart, just that: the perfect Halloween, blown away in one second. Dreams, these days, can do that. Break my heart. But there's worse to come: I wake up and there's Br'er Bertrand. He's some kind of clergy-nerd. I don't know his denomination and, anyway, I call all of the religious types Br'er Whatever. Even the women. To me, that has just the ring of contempt that I wish to convey to the representatives of Somebody Up There without being totally disrespectful. Some of them laugh.

Bertrand is sitting by my bed, has probably been there for hours while I was innocently asleep. In a sneak attack, there he's been, mumbling over my rat-ass soul. I groan and turn my back, hunching over in the bed, fake-retching. But he keeps on muttering.

"Get out, dude," I moan. "I told you, I don't want to talk to you. Leave me alone. I'm sick." Worth a try, I suppose, even though I know that this Br'er is not easily discouraged. And I have a deep suspicion that my mom asked him to check on me while she can't come in. Him and about nine different counselors and whatnot. She isn't missing a trick, flu or not.

So I'm not a whole lot surprised when the man goes, "No, Richard. God hasn't left you, and neither will I."

I roll over and open one eye, all I can bear. Bertrand is about thirty-five years old and he's the slobbiest man I ever met. I mean, his black coat and white collar always look like someone finger-painted scrambled egg all over them, and he's pale and pasty and big-time fat, and he's got fingers like short white worms. And bright red hair sticking up out of a bright pink scalp. Sweartogod, it's like having some pudgy, grubby clown show up at your bedside first thing in the morning. In the Real World, no one would put up with this, not for three freaking seconds. If this was a hotel, somebody would call the manager and have the guy tossed out on his ass. Somebody would scream for the cops and the men in the white coats. Headlines would read: LUNATIC INVADES PRIVATE ROOM, INFLICTS UNWANTED PRAYER WHILE GUY SLEEPS. CRUCIFIX AND BIBLE USED AS WEAPONS.

But here? No. Here, on Halloween morning no less, the lunatic sits in a green plastic chair, his butt cheeks squeezing out either side, and smiles up at me in my high bed. And there is fuck-all I can do about it. I'm helpless in my steel-rail cage.

So, ole Bertrand looks up from his black book and says, "You created a very nasty scene last night."

29

I just glare.

"First of all," he goes on, ignoring the death ray stare I'm aiming at his pink skull, "it is risky business to invite Satan into your life, even in play. Satan does not play. He's waiting, every second of the day. Your costume and your attitude yesterday afternoon were foolish." He shakes his head and shafts of orange hair shift on his scalp. "Why, I have to wonder, would anyone in your position risk bringing evil into your life? Why, I wonder, would you invite that poor sweet girl to join you in your folly?"

I open the other eye. Double death ray glare. "Hey, you know what, Br'er?" I rasp out. "You're right. Absolutely correct. You're a genius. You guessed it, and it actually happened. Yes, sir, the devil himself visited my room last night. Breathed fire and brimstone right into my face. And you know what I did? I punched him in the face." I hold up my bandaged knuckles. "Beat his butt, fair and square. So my soul is safe, man. You can go save somebody else. I think that wily Mrs. Elkins—you know, that old broad in room 301?—she's been running drugs from her room. Crack, heroin, all kinds of shit. And there was a séance in there the other night, stroke of midnight. Ouija board, black candles, inverted pentagrams, the whole nine yards. She's, like, invoking demons right and left. You better talk to her." This is actually very funny, if you know about Mrs.

Elkins—she's, like, ninety-two and hasn't been conscious even once since I've been here. She's tiny and wrapped in white sheets all the time; she's like this little cocoon thing attached to her bed. I mean, no one would look in there and think *human being,* not in a million years. Except that her son—so presumably she once had a kid, ergo was a living, breathing woman who had sex and everything, it simply blows the mind to imagine that—wanders around here, impatient and cranky. Anyway, the notion of Mrs. Elkins as a one-woman devil-worshipping drug cartel is pretty brilliant. But I don't really expect Bertrand to appreciate my wit.

He doesn't. Luckily, he gets mad, all huffy. That's the best that can happen: if you piss them off, they leave. Although later, they often feel bad that they let a dying kid annoy them and they come back, all contrition and penance, even worse than all self-righteous, like they need *you* to give *them* absolution. But, for now, this Br'er shakes his head and puts his finger in my face. "You're treading very thin ice, son," he says. "Very, very thin." And then his fat butt wobbles out of my room and I get about eleven minutes' peace before Edward shows up with my breakfast tray.

Now here's another thing: like I told you, I don't eat. And I told the food service people that, too, and then I told them again. I made it very clear: don't even bring the slop to my room. But three times a day, up shows a tray. Full of all sorts of disgusting crap. Today, it's chartreuse scrambled eggs, greasy sausage, soggy toast, vitamin-laced pudding, green Jell-O, custard, and this stuff that's called thickened juice, i.e., fruit punch that you can spoon up, like some kind of cruel mockery of a Slurpee. But, praise be, there's also a cup of hot coffee—and that's my only salvation. I allow myself to put sugar and milk in the coffee, too. My one concession to caloric intake.

Edward doesn't even bother to put the rest of the swill on my bed table. He just hands over the coffee, which I have to hold in my left hand because of my bandaged knuckles. Edward rolls his eyes, looking at my wrapped-up hand, but he doesn't say a word about it. He just bustles around, straightening things up, then says, "You going to shower, young Richard? Or do you want to wash up in bed?"

I have to think about it. It's actually a big decision, believe it or not. It's a huge hassle to get clean around here. But it's kind of a point of pride for me to get up, every lousy day, and let water run all over my body. I don't know why—I don't sweat anymore, and I don't think that I stink. But it's my own little baptism, I guess. Or just my own tip of the hat to normal. So I usually do it.

And here's the weird thing, that I'd hate for my old high school buddies—like, all three of them, popularity not being top of my résumé—to know: I only like Edward to give me my shower. And, yes, he's gay. (No, he never told me this—it's just pretty obvious.) So what does that mean? I could worry, I suppose, about this showering preference, but I don't. Because I know exactly where it comes from.

See, back in one of the other hospitals when I was about fifteen, I got bed-bathed once by the prettiest nurse on the onco-surgo floor. One of the 18 percent of non-fat nurses. Young. Cute little freckles on her nose and a body that strained against that polyester uniform material in all the right places. And she was sweet. Anybody can guess where this is leading, for sure. Humiliation nation, that's where. Seems a bit funny, now. Seemed like absolute end-of-the-world then. Anyway, I'm lying on my back, tied down by IVs and chest drains and all kinds of hospital bondage devices, and there *she* is, running a warm soapy washcloth over my feet and calves. And she's just chattering away like they do to keep you from being embarrassed—telling me some silly story about her best friend's baby shower where there was the *cutest* set of onesies and the most *adorable* teddy bear. And her hair is kind of honey-brown, long and curly, and she keeps having to push a strand behind one ear. ("Why don't nurses wear caps anymore?" my mom asked once, pointing at all that gorgeous hair. "Isn't that unsanitary?" Who cares? I thought. I crave her bacteria.) Now usually, the nurses stop the washcloth just above the knees or so and ask if you want to wash your own private parts—or they just ignore that whole area. But this is one thorough bather. Some head nurse has told her to wash me up, and by jiminy, this girl is going to *wash*, bless her.

So she keeps on chatting—"there were the *sweetest* bouncy seats and little blue blankets," blah de blah—and that washcloth is climbing up my thighs like a warm tongue. Or what I imagine one of those would feel like— imagination being all I've got to go on. And, of course, I get a boner like the Washington Monument, and that stops the nurse flat. She can't help but let out one totally unprofessional giggle and a nicely complimentary (I like to think) "Whoa there!" And then she steps back, puts the washcloth very gently into my hand, and she says, soft as she can, eyes down on the floor, trying not to smile, you can tell, "Well then, Richard. Tell you what. I think I'll leave you to finish up here alone." She closes the bed curtains really tight behind her as she flees my little hormonally charged tent. "You just ring when you're done."

Well, what are you going to do? I'll tell you what I wanted to do. I wanted to beg and plead and bribe her to come back. I wanted to ring the emergency buzzer and force her to come back. I wanted her to understand that this was a medical emergency, by all that's holy. Take care of me, nurse, please.

But, no. Wasn't going to happen, I knew that. So I did what she told me. I finished up alone.

So now I try to avoid all such incidents. Although I don't even know, really, how well ole Bingo works anymore. I mean, I was relatively strong, even post-op, at fifteen. Now, at the advanced age of seventeen-going-on-eighteen, I'm a mere ghost of my former horny self. Still, I think it's wise to only let guy nurses bathe me. It's better, all around. And Edward is usually the only guy on mornings. But that's cool, because he's about 6'4" and probably goes close to three hundred pounds: another strong one. And he's fast and gentle and he doesn't chatter at you. Gives a nice efficient, no-fuss shower.

Anyway, I'll skip the stupid problems of even getting into the shower when you're all weak and wobbly and the horrors of sitting your bare ass on one of those little white plastic bathing stools where your balls always get squinched into one of the idiotically placed drainage-hole perforation things. It's pathetically comic, for sure, but it gets a bit old as a daily event. What's important is that, while I'm in there, hunched on that silly stool, shampoo on my fuzzed-over (grown back from bald, like, three times now) head, with Edward scrubbing my back (the dude wisely ignores all the dangling-down parts), I hear a loud voice in the hall. It's yelling, "Hey, where's King Richard the First, goddamn it? Somebody tell him his old uncle's here to visit, will you? Tell him it's time for trick or treat."

And my whole day changes. Because I'd know that voice anywhere. That's my Uncle Phil, my mom's no-good, black-sheep, crazy-ass baby brother. And, all of a sudden, this particular Halloween brightens right up.

4

I YELL OUT, RIGHT from the shower room, "Hey, Uncle Phil, in here." And Edward just has time to throw a washcloth over my crotch, and then the whole steamy little room is full of Phil, who smells like bacon and marijuana smoke and outdoors air—sort of like my idea of paradise, in other words. I try to sit up tall in my chair and I try, I don't know exactly, to puff up, make myself look bigger and stronger, and I know I have a big old grin on my face when Phil first catches a glimpse of me.

Phil's sneakers slide right out from under him, and he ends up sitting on his ass on the wet floor. For a second or so, the man puts his face into his hands and slumps there, still as a statue. That's when I get a real-life view of my hero: he's a couple years younger than Mom, so that makes him just over thirty. But he looks middle-aged, sitting there with his head bowed. He's got a perfectly round bald spot on the back of his head, like some alien-created crop circle lurking in his mess of brown curls. And he's—well, I got to say it, he's dumpy. He's got a round pot of belly plopping over the fancy silver buckle of his cowboy belt. But the guy's got spirit, you know? Because after giving in to just that tiny bit of wimpiness, he rallies. Phil looks up and he's got even a bigger smile than I have, even if his eyes are all teary. And he flips onto his knees and does this little knightly bow in front of my chair, swinging an imaginary hat off his head and bowing at the waist. "Your humble servant, King Richard," he says. "Kneeling at your royal feet."

That's Uncle Phil, all over. Always has some game going on. I mean, I think that's him. I don't really know a whole lot about him. Mom kept him at arm's length—or more like five arms' length—for most of my life. I'd just hear the stories she'd pick up over the phone from her mom in Jersey, where Phil moved back in with Grandma, right after I was born. Over the years, they piled up, those phone-call tales: Phil lost his license again; Phil called from the city lockup; Phil got some girl pregnant; the girl went and got an abortion; Phil went and sat outside the clinic, crying like a lost dog; Phil dropped out of community college, three credits short of a degree; Phil got married; Phil got divorced; Phil got fired; Phil got sued; Phil got in a bar fight; Phil got thirty-one stitches; Phil this;

Phil that. When I was little, I just heard his name churning through those late-night phone calls. I'd lie there in my bed in the dark and listen to my mom's reactions. She was always half laughing, half crying. She'd keep saying things like, "Oh *no*. Not again. *Un*believable. Is he *crazy?*" And on and on it would go, until it all kind of meshed in with my dreams. I secretly thought my uncle Phil must be the coolest guy ever.

I finally met him a couple of times when I was older, around thirteen or so. Bang, one day he just showed up at the New York City hospital where I was an inmate, said he wanted to cheer me up. And he kept on showing up, on and off, ever after. Always brought some forbidden present: green slime in a tube, Fritos when I wasn't allowed to eat even Jell-O, magazines with bare-chested babes on the cover. Once, an entire badminton set—like anyone was going to let me set up the net by the nurses' station and belt birdies all over the hallway. Mom always told him to get lost, and she swore she didn't know how he found out where we were, said she sure as shit didn't tell him, but she also always had a smile on her face and she always hugged him, hard, before smacking him upside the head and calling him the world's biggest jerk.

Now, here in the steamed-up shower room, everything seems all backward. Because when Uncle Phil does his "your humble servant" thing and gets on his knees in front of me and is damn near kissing my feet, I get the whole view of his little bald spot—and right then, I get something: I know he doesn't know it's there. He hasn't got a clue. It's one of those stealth baldnesses, the kind that you can't see yourself without two mirrors, so you live on in happy ignorance unless a mean girlfriend or barber points it out. And somehow, I figure that makes us sort of even: me all puny and sick, and him getting old and bald and not even realizing it. Because I won't ever have to go through that, will I? Once, I made a list of all the things I won't have to worry about—getting a job, having ungrateful kids, divorce, wisdom teeth, cholesterol—and now I can add potbelly and comb-overs, and in its own weird way, that's cool with me.

Edward is looking on in what I hope is amusement, but he does have work to do and he can't hang with us all day. "Hey, man," he says to Phil. "We don't usually welcome visitors in the shower. You want to wait in the lounge until King Richard here is robed and ready to receive callers?"

And Phil, who can really get into a scenario, backs all the way out the door, bowing and sweeping his pretend hat across the floor and tripping all over his feet. "Verily, my liege lord," he says. "Anon."

When the door swings shut behind him, I feel like

Edward deserves an explanation, and I try to think of how to explain Phil, but it doesn't matter. Because Edward just starts pulling a clean T-shirt over my head and says, "Maybe you want to wear jeans today? Instead of your usual granny pants?" He holds up the ratty pair of gray sweats I usually put on because who cares what covers your ass when your ass sits in a wheelchair or lies in bed all day? And I nod and he goes off to fetch a pair of clean jeans from my room. I mean, he got it, right off, that I want to look, like, human and normal for Uncle Phil. Really, Edward's a prince among nurses, and if I had my way, they'd double his pay.

When he gets back and we've wrestled my sorry self into my jeans, I actually take a minute to look into the shower room mirror. Don't usually bother but, I don't know, I'd kind of like to look okay today. And, dressed, I look like a skinny bald scarecrow, but that's not really so bad. Short-to-the-point-of-nothing hair is sort of in style, and everybody's jeans are three sizes too big, so that's okay. Granted, my face is not a sight for sissies. No eyelashes, skin like chalk dust. No problemo. I'm feeling okay, all kind of buzzed, full of energy. Edward stands over my shoulder while I look, trying to reach down and rebandage my hand. But I hold it up to the mirror and say, "Hey. Leave it alone, okay? It looks cool. Tough, right?"

41

The knuckles are all blue and there's an impressive mess of half-open cuts all along there, kind of oozy and gross. And actually, the bruising runs right up to my arm, and there's a very flashy blackish sort of zigzag going up from pinky to wrist. Looks like a negative of lightning, like a prison tat. I love it.

Edward is muttering that I should have had my arm x-rayed, could have broken that little bone.

"Let it go, man," I say. "No intervention. Okay?"

"Right. And if you get an infection in there, who's in trouble? Me, that's who." He glares at me in the mirror. "Flesh-eating bacteria, Richard. Staph. Strep. MRSA. C. diff. There's nasty stuff out there. No sirree. I'm treating that hand." And he just starts slathering antibiotic cream all over it and has it rewrapped in gauze in about four seconds.

I hold it up in the mirror again. All wrapped like that, I decide, it's still cool. Like Rocky the morning after. I can live with it.

I get rolled back into my room, and Phil's lying on the bed, his dirty sneakers right on the clean sheets an aide put on there while I was in the shower. I see his eyes go right to the bandage. So, of course, I got to tell him all about it. How the devil himself came into my room, and how I punched out his lights. Sent him reeling right on back to hell. Doused his flames with a good right hook.

Phil laughs and laughs. "That's my boy," he says and holds up his own right hand. The knuckles are permanently bruised, looks like, and there's a big bump on that same little pinky wrist bone. He shakes the hand around like a dust mop. "This puppy has been busted about eight times. Lots of sore jaws on lots of big, mean Jersey jerks, let me tell you." He jumps off the bed and leans over me, both his hands up in fists. Then we do that sort of fake boxing thing—the one with punches that never land. I get out of breath real fast, just holding my arms up. But it's fun anyway—two tough dudes just messing around.

***

Later, I give Phil a tour of the place, because he seems honestly interested. Maybe a bit too much so; maybe some of it's a kind of twisted nosiness, because I can't get him to understand that gaping at the patients and gasping are not exactly acceptable in Miss Manners' Rules of Hospice Etiquette. But I try to really show him the place, try to make him *see* it. Because he's the only one I know who seems willing; most folks try not to look or just refuse to see. Mom, for example, pretends that it's any old hospital ward, like we've been in and out of a gazillion times before. In and *out* of. See? That's the key: all the other hospitals had a way out, and I walked, eventually. But this place, it's like *No Exit*, a pretty cool play they made me read in some English class. And most people are all for not seeing—not *letting* themselves see—that this is different, a whole nother world. A whole universe, and it's important, in some way I can't really get at in words. I mean, it's the Last Stop, and that alone makes it Big—significant, you know? Me, I'm dying to show it off—ha ha.

I start at the back end of the hall. "Family lounge to your right," I say. Phil's pushing my chair, but he keeps stopping, leaving me to sit still while he steps off to look inside places. So off he goes, into the family lounge. It is not much, let me tell you. One wall has kitchen-y stuff—coffeepot, microwave, fridge, and a counter with a mess of straws and Sweet 'n Low and sticky plastic spoons all over it. And there are a couple of lumpy couches where people can sleep. A round table in the middle of the room, with a chess set and decks of cards. Bathroom in the corner. Dusty old plastic flower arrangements all over the place. Pictures of lakes and streams and oceans and waterfalls—somebody must think water is soothing or something—on the walls. But, trust Phil, he gloms on to the TV set and the stack of DVDs next to it. He picks them up and starts shuffling through. I know what he's reading, and I watch his face. The titles are all, like, *Good-bye Is Not Forever, Easing the Ending, Beyond the Far Horizon, God Doesn't Make*

44

Mistakes, et cetera. Believe me, I checked them out the day I got here, hoping for entertainment. Ha. Although I have got to say, *God Doesn't Make Mistakes* really confirmed the SUTHY diagnosis: six years of chemo, radiation, a zillion surgeries, loss of a couple major organs, watching your mom age twenty years in twenty months—if that's not some kind of *mistake*, if that's part of the Big Dude's *plan*, well, then, it's pretty obvious, isn't it? Enough said.

Anyway, Phil is shaking his head. "What pathetic crap," he says. And then he brightens up. "Tell you what, kiddo. Next time I'm in, I'm bringing some good old-fashioned porn. Slip *Debbie Does Disney World* inside one of these lame covers: surprise! Make some guy's night."

We proceed along the hall. Doesn't take long. There are five rooms on the east side of the hall to our left, three doubles and two singles. Each room is a different color, all of these cheesy pastels. And each one has its own individual wallpaper border up near the ceiling, all of these dingy flowery things. Right out of 1970s home decor magazines, my mom says. They're supposed to make the rooms feel cozy or something. Un-hospitalish, I guess is the concept. But trust me. They don't. You can't mistake a hospital room for anything else in the whole world. Except maybe a jail cell.

Anyway, right now, two double rooms are empty. One

of the singles, 306, right across from me, has a woman in a coma in it. Her walls are light blue, and her border is, sweartogod, little flying cherub babies, with wings and fat toes, sort of hovering over her, looking down. Pretty disturbing. I tell Phil, in the customary hospice whisper, what I heard about her: She was in a coma after a car accident for years and years, ventilator, feeding tubes, the whole shebang, kept in place by her husband. Then the husband dropped dead and her daughters, finally, got to have all the tubes removed and the machines turned off. Plugs pulled, zappo, end of story. Right? Wrong. The woman kept right on breathing. Although they can't expect her to go much longer; you only get into hospice if your prognosis is under a month. Phil goes right into the woman's room and puts his face an inch from hers. He stares until I hiss, "Phil, that's rude. Get *out* of there. Come on."

Then he takes up his wheelchair post, scratching at his stubbly cheeks. "I hate to disappoint anybody, but that lady is stone cold dead, man, breathing or not," he observes. And off we go.

Next, there's the two old guys in 304. Yellow walls, rose border. These two never have visitors, have no story that I know of. Nada. Now, to me, that's sad. Couple of times, late at night, I rolled on in there and watched TV with them. The one by the window, he likes to have soccer on the tube, so that's what I put on. Can't follow the game, myself, but he seems to like it, curses one team, cheers the other. The other guy, I don't know. Doesn't say a word, just coughs. Phil leans into the doorway, gives the guys a jaunty little "howdy" kind of wave, but they're both sound asleep.

Now we get to 302 and I get real nervous, because this is Sylvie. And her mother's in there with the three little boys, and I think I'm probably, like, persona non whatever in there today. So I say, "Let's not bother her, okay? She's tired."

Of course, I told Phil all about Sylvie and our Cabbage Night prank earlier, kind of bragging, I'll admit, and he thought it was great, so he understands that the girl is exhausted. But he just trots on in anyway. I stay way back in the hallway, but I can hear him talking to the boys, all jolly uncle-like, and then he says something that actually makes Sylvie's mom laugh, and I think, shit, he's *flirting* with her. And I think how completely and totally pissed Sylvie's father would be about that, and that's a happy thought. So I roll myself just into the doorway and check it out. Sylvie herself is totally invisible, just a series of small lumps in her bed, covers pulled up over her head. I see Phil looking at the photos they've got plastered all over the walls, and I know what every one looks like, since I memorized them all: Sylvie in her private school uniform; Sylvie on the swim team, all long legs and nice round boobs in a stretchy suit; Sylvie going to some dance in a fancy pink dress, white flowers pinned to her newly blooming chest; Sylvie as a black-haired, brown-eyed baby; Sylvie with a bunch of her friends, all the boys tall and handsome, all the girls shiny-haired and cute; Sylvie getting some award; Sylvie on the front porch of a big white house, twin baby brothers on her lap; Sylvie at the beach, tan and glowing; Sylvie, Sylvie, Sylvie. They're there, all those pictures, a record, so that everyone who steps into that room—which is a color Sylvie calls puke pink—will know that somewhere inside that yellow-skinned, bag-of-bones, bald-headed Sylvie is that other one: cool, popular, smart, nice house, nice family. And pretty. Really.

When Uncle Phil comes out of her room, that's all he says. "Pretty girl." And his voice is all rough and shaky.

Our next stop is the little lobby by the elevator, and here Phil stops dead. He's staring at the harpy, who's just setting up for the day. Phil leans over my shoulder and breathes, "What the fuck?" into my ear.

I raise one finger. "Exactamundo. Just wait," I say.

The harpy, who today has her creepy white hair loose on her shoulders like a frizzy cloud, smiles at us. "Welcome, Richard," she whispers. (She always whispers. That ups the weirdness quotient a notch, I say.) She settles herself on the little stool thing. She's got on a long fuzzy skirt, black, with a shiny white blouse. She closes her eyes and raises her hands—long, crooked, creepy fingers—to the strings.

"Just wait," I say again to Phil, soft. "Here it comes."

But the harpy's eyes spring back open and she smiles, dropping her hands. "Happy Halloween, Richard," she says. And she reaches into one of the pockets in that black skirt and brings up a package of Good & Plenty. "I believe you're allowed candy." She tosses that little pink-and-black-and-white box into my lap, then lifts her hands to the harp, shuts her eyes, and starts to strum. The lobby fills up with sweet, sad sounds.

Phil's hands jerk on the handles of the chair, and before you can say "Jack Robinson" (that's an expression my grandma always says), we're gone, backed right up into our hallway, wheels up against the nurses' station. He stops and picks the Good & Plenty out of my lap with two fingers, like it was laced with arsenic or something, and drops it on the counter. He opens it up and pours out the little pink and white lozenges that look like pills. "Do not eat those, my liege," he says. "Good & Plenty has been known to kill perfectly healthy monarchs. This was sent by your enemies." He raises his voice and addresses the floor clerk,

Mrs. Lee, a woman in her fifties who's mean and cranky with everybody, but who, I heard, cries like a baby whenever they wheel one of us, covered head to toe with a white sheet, out the doors. Since this is a near-daily occurrence, the woman keeps a huge box of Kleenex at her side. The rest of the time, she's universally rude, and that seems fair to me. Phil leans over and says to her, "That apparition in the lobby gave my nephew a box of these, these . . . items. For Halloween, she said." He pokes a finger into the pile of candy. "Clearly, she is a servant of"—he lowers his voice and hisses—"what I will call only the Lower Regions."

Mrs. Lee eyes the Good & Plenty, and she eyes Phil. Then she picks up one of the little pink pills and puts it in her mouth and chews it up, smiling wide with licorice-blackened teeth. "The white ones will kill you," she says. "Pink ones are yummy."

I laugh—the woman's all right, and she's left Phil speechless, which is not easy.

After that, the rest of our tour is quick, just the west side of the hall. My side. Mrs. Elkins in 301, two old women in 303, another old woman in 307—and in 305, *moi*. I don't know why I'm the only guy on what seems to be the female side. When I asked Edward, he shrugged and said, "Doesn't matter. The rooms change all the time." And then he sort of blushed, because he realized what that meant. Out with the dead, in with the dying. The king is dead, long live the king.

My room, I have to say, isn't the absolute worst in terms of color or border. It's what my mom calls mauve, and the border, she says, that's lilacs and violets and ivy, all looped all over one another. It's springy, she says. I don't much notice, most of the time. Except at night, when I can't sleep and I'm looking up at all those bunches of flowers, just hanging there on the wall. I wish they'd, like, wither or something. I mean, change, somehow. It's not right when things stay exactly the same, day after day. Sometimes I think about all the other people who've slept—or not—in this bed and looked at those damn lilacs. But mostly I don't think about them. What's the use?

Phil sits down on my bed, staring out the window for a minute, kind of quiet. But then he says, "Great view." And, you know, it is—that's the whole beauty of the west side and the main reason I'm happy I got put here. We're at the top of the hill, and the city of Hudson runs right down to the river. I can see all the way down Warren Street and, on a clear fall day like today, the river sparkles all blue and clean down there. Up close, believe me, the Hudson is not so sparkly. But from up here it is. And behind it, the Catskill Mountains rise up, darker blue and curvy on top. Look at those mountains like that, against the sky, and you

51

see the shape of a naked woman on her back. I'm not making that up—everybody sees it. In fact, it was my mom who pointed it out, long time back. The Catskill woman, she's lying down, and the mountains to the south are her hair, all sort of spread out. Then there's her face, profile, sort of turned away, toward the west. Then her breasts, clear as day, two nice pointy ones. Then a sort of dip—her belly. And then two raised-up, bent knees. Like she's lying there, all open and ready, like some sort of sky god or something is going to come down and make her day.

Mom always said the Catskills were, like, magical, that the Indians who used to live there way back, they thought the mountains were sort of sacred or something. And the whole valley, it's Sleepy Hollow country. All of it, kind of haunted. Mom used to make up stories to tell me, especially this time of year, to scare my socks off. But from up here, it doesn't look scary. It's real pretty, actually. Church steeples and all that red brick and stone of the old buildings, like a painting.

Hudson has been around forever, and I'm glad that I get to see it from kind of above, you know? All stretched out, all the people who built the buildings and the churches and the railroad tracks and the boats—all long dead. That's what I think about lots of times when I look out this window. Every one of them, dead. And new ones coming along every day. The maternity ward, all those newbie humans, that's right above my head, fourth floor. (Where I myself put in my first appearance, I'd like to note, seventeen years ago.) The morgue? I guess that's in the basement. Like our sign said: *Going down. This means you.* One of the therapists told me that's why he can keep on working here, that's what we all need to understand: the long view. I think about that for a while and we're quiet, me and Phil, taking in the sights.

And then Phil says three interesting things. First, that he's going to make a drawing, soon as he gets home, like a map or sketch, of this hospice and how the city rolls away from it, right down to the river. And how the river rolls away to the ocean. He's going to put in all the rooms and all the occupants, and he's going to put me in my wheelchair right in the middle of the hallway, sort of in the foreground, watching it all, inside and out, and he's going to call it *Richie's World*. And I know that he means it, and I know that that's one thing Phil has always been good at: he can draw. My mom keeps a couple of his drawings on her bedroom wall in frames, ones he did when he was in high school. Cows in a field. A train, coming right at you, funny angle, like you're tied to the tracks. And a portrait of my mom at seventeen, wide eyes, funny little smile, me still a secret inside her. Phil's drawings won all the Hudson

High awards. So I'm sure that *Richie's World* will be very cool.

Second, he says, "So what do you *do* around here, my man? I mean, where's your computer, your music, your entertainment center? Okay, there's a TV, but what else?"

I don't want to tell him this, but I don't e-mail and I don't text anymore because, real simple, I don't see all that well these days. I mean, it's just one more thing he doesn't need to know, that when you get to this point, your eyes don't work so hot. And screens, all that light and movement, they're really painful and, I don't know, unstable or something. All flickery and weird. Video games—all those flashy colors—they're like torture. Like you're not on the outside anymore, but got sucked all the way in, where the explosions happen inside your skull. And it's just plain impossible for me to read words on any screen anymore. Even print on a page, it jumps around and makes you want to puke.

But I don't say any of that, don't bother to explain. See, there's a whole lot of stuff you learn in here that you don't necessarily feel you should pass on to the world. Like how sunlight hurts our eyes and how, overall, this whole process is like being hollowed out. Like a cantaloupe or something, you know, after someone's metal spoon has been in there, scraping out all the good stuff—all the fruit and juice. Like what's left is just shell, you know? The rind. So I say to Phil, "Hey, man, I'm entertained by the whole human comedy, that's all. Live-action. There's always something happening here. It's a riot." And it's funny—that's almost true. I don't miss cyberspace at all.

After a few minutes of thinking about that, Phil says the third interesting thing. "Richard, my liege. You definitely need to get out more. How'd you like to spend Halloween night out in the Real World? Hit some hot spots, pick up chicks, trick or treat? Let's blow this joint, man."

And you'd think I'd be jumping for joy, right? I mean, a night out with Uncle Phil? My mother not around to say no? That's like a lifetime fantasy come true. But what I feel is more scared than anything else. I haven't been out in a long time. And I'm not so sure I can handle the Real World. Or it can handle me. See, around here, no one winces at how we look—there are no scars too horrible to bear. It's all *normal* here to be hideous. I hate to be a wuss, though, in front of Phil. So I'm waffling when the phone rings.

I say, "Hi, Ma, how you feeling?" and I watch as Phil waves his hands and shakes his head, the classic *I am not here* gesture. I nod: right, he's not here. Like I said, phoning is not seeing, is it?

MOM'S VOICE IS ALL hoarse and low. Hard to say if that's from the flu or from crying, which she does whenever she thinks I can't see her. It hits me that, this week at home, the woman is probably in tears about 98 percent of the time, and I feel pretty lousy that I've been enjoying myself so much. "Hey, Ma," I say, "you okay?"

There's one loud, throat-clearing hack and then she says, "Sweetie, I'm fine. You?"

"Fine. Doing good." This is my standard lie. There's absolutely no sense saying anything else, because if you do, you have to get all into it, and that's just repetitive and boring.

"I'm so worried that you're lonely. Anybody been in to see you?"

I close my eyes and try to come up with some version of the truth. "A couple of counselors. One of the Br'ers. Oh, yeah, Sylvie's dad."

There's surprise in her voice. "Sylvie's dad? He's not usually a sociable man, I've got to say. Why did he . . . Oh, god. Is Sylvie . . .?"

That question pisses me right off. I want to scream: *Is Sylvie what? Where? Sylvie?* I just cannot go there. "Shit, Ma. Sylvie's fine, okay? She's *fine*. Listen, I got to go take a shower. Talk to you later." I'm short of breath and I can feel my heart pounding in my ears. I get all dizzy and have to lean back on my pillows.

Phil's been listening, not even pretending not to. He takes the phone out of my hand and clicks it shut. "Mothers, huh? What a pain in the ass." He frowns. "So, Sisco have anything interesting to say?"

Sisco is Phil's name for my mother, his big sister. I shake my head, not enough breath to speak.

Phil slides up the bed until he's sitting right next to me. We're both leaning on the pillows now. "Hey, man, forget it." He nudges me with his elbow. "I bet there's good Halloween stuff on TV. Like, Monster Movie Marathon or something."

So that's what we do, all afternoon: watch old horror flicks on TCM. There are the silly ones, the stupid ones and the ones that scare your socks off. Like *The Haunting*— the old one, that is, not that new piece-of-crap version. No, this is the one where this woman named Eleanor—Nell, they call her—is, like, half nuts, half sane. Half in love with Hill House, half scared as shit. The house wins. The last thing she says, driving straight into a tree, is "Why don't they stop me?" Jeez Louise. Mom and me, we read the book, *The Haunting of Hill House,* together when I was about twelve. We had to read it together because we were both too scared to read it alone. We'd sit on my bed—I was hooked up to IVs, even at home, every night, long story, not worth going into—and we'd read, silently, turning a page only when both of us were done with it. Then we went on to *We Have Always Lived in the Castle.* That Shirley Jackson, man, she can throw a lump of pure darkness into your chest, you know? She can spin your head around and make you totally, like, off balance. But I got to say that, looking back, those were sweet times for Mom and me. I was home, we were scared together, not alone. Kind of nice, really.

The supper tray comes at five. I've got such a headache from TV overload that I can't even look at it. Phil makes fake gagging sounds, pointing at the food. But he sits down and eats it all while I sip the coffee. Then he claps his hands and says, "Okay, my liege, your food taster has declared this safe for your consumption." He waves at the empty tray, and we both laugh like hyenas. He paces around the room a few times, looks out the window and puts his hands on his hips. "It's time to go, pal." He makes his voice all dramatic and fake spooky: "As darkness falls on the city of Hudson this hallowed night, strange figures appear on the streets. Children in costume? Or the denizens of the deep, showing their true faces? Who really knows? Who can really tell innocence from evil on this Halloween night?" He gives a long, loud, monstrous laugh: "*Bwaaaa, ha, ha, ha.*"

There's applause from the doorway. Jeannette's back on duty and she's smiling. In fact, she's got a funny, shy kind of look in her eyes. "My god, it's Philip Casey," she says. "I haven't seen your ugly face since, what, freshman year of high school? Fancy running into you here."

Phil looks at her for a few ticks. She's big, like I said, but she's attractive and she's got a real spark, tonight at least. She's wearing a uniform top with smiling jack-o'-lanterns all over it. Suddenly, this hits me: it's the first time in all my whole life that me and Mom didn't carve one. For a second, it's all there in my head: the newspapers on the kitchen table, the knife in my hand. The deep cut around the stem, careful not to damage the stem, then the tugging off of the top of the pumpkin. It's right there: the orange-gold of the innards and the smell, sharp as anything, of pumpkin guts on my hands. The clumsy triangle eyes and fangs we always went for. That great moment when Mom lit the candle inside and, bammo, the thing came to life. And the taste of the seeds, roasted in our oven and covered with salt. I can feel tears stinging my eyes, and I'm glad that Phil and Jeannette are too busy looking at each other to pay me any mind.

"Jeannie?" Phil's got a big ole grin on his face. "Oh man. Jeannie. Long time, girl. I had no idea you worked here."

Jeannette comes all the way into the room, sashaying her hips. "Well, I didn't know that you know our Richard," she said. "Didn't put the names together 'til right this minute."

"Know him? *Know* him? Hey, I'm his uncle. I'm family. We are both Casey men. We're tight. Aren't we, my man?"

Tight, me and Phil? I wish it were true, so I try to smile. "Yep."

Phil goes over and gives Jeannette a hug. "Listen, Jeannie," he says, right in her ear. "Can you, maybe, just not check on our man Richard here? For a couple hours, maybe?"

She pulls back and frowns. "Not check on a patient? I don't think so."

Phil smooths his hand along her back. "Honey," he says, soft and sweet. "This is a seventeen-year-old kid we got here. Remember what it was like, being seventeen? It's

Halloween night. I'll take care of him, I promise. Don't you allow, like, little leaves of absence? When accompanied by a responsible adult?"

She snorts. "Yeah, sure. And who might that be?"

His voice gets even softer. Maybe he thinks I can't hear him. But that's where he's wrong. The best sense I got these days is hearing. It's sharp as can be. "He's a *kid*," he says. "And this is his last Halloween."

I shut my eyes, hard. I don't even know if I'm rooting for him to convince her or not. I don't have the energy right now to plan a breakout. He's the adult—let him do it.

Jeannette's voice is thick and quiet. "Shoot. All right. Two hours. You got two hours. If that boy isn't in his bed, safe and sound, by nine o'clock, I'm calling the state troopers and the county sheriff, both. You got it?"

I let my eyes flick open. Holy moly—she went for it. Phil really is a magician.

Phil kisses her cheek and she stamps out of the room, shaking her head, but smiling. Then he runs around out in the hall and comes back with scissors and some pieces of construction paper. He hunches over the bed table for a few minutes, cutting and folding, then he leaps up and he's got a crown in his hand, like the kind they used to give out at Burger King. And he fusses around, fitting it on my head and taping it together in back. He pulls a little black mask—the Zorro kind—out of his pocket and fits it around my face, elastic snapping in back. Then he takes the blanket off the bottom of the bed—the nice fuzzy one Mom brings to every hospital, dark blue with little gold stars all over it—and he drapes it around my shoulders, like a cape. He pushes my hospital bracelet way up my arm, invisible under the cape. Together, we unwrap the bandages on my hand, which looks nicely badass. He steps back and then smiles and bows. "My lord," he says. "Your disguise is complete. And your humble servant begs your leave to get you *outta* here."

I nod. "You got it, man. Let's go."

How we get out is so simple, I'm surprised I never did it myself. No one says boo as we go down the hallway and into the lobby. (The harpy, thankfully, has closed down for the night.) I sit up straight in the wheelchair, crown on my head, and Phil pushes from behind. He smiles and nods at everyone we pass. He hits the down button for the elevator, and when the doors open, there's Mrs. Elkins's son stepping out. He looks a little surprised, but he holds the doors open for us.

It takes him a minute, but then he recognizes me. "Going out, Richard?" he asks.

I wink, but that's useless behind my mask, so I give him a big grin. "Got a hot date, Mr. E," I say. "Happy Halloween."

The look on the guy's face is just, I don't know, weird.

Once we're inside the elevator, Phil and I start to hoot. But it's not until we make it through a whole bunch of corridors and right on out the big glass doors at the front of the hospital that I really believe it. Not until we're actually outside, in the cool October air, does it seem even a little bit real. It's the air that does it: I haven't been out in I don't know how long—came straight from the big New York hospital, by ambulance, to this one.

Outside, it's amazing. And it's a perfect night: just a little cool, just a little breeze, clouds skimming through the sky, leaves rustling along the curbs. I get goose bumps all up my shins as that air hits my skin. I take in big gulps of it. And there's noise: buses, cars, kids whooping and hollering somewhere—life noises. Real World noises. And smells: Exhaust, dead leaves, wetness from the storm drains, and beyond all that, the river. The Hudson, moving along down there, slow and deep and full of strong currents. It's always been there, all my life, that river smell. But I never really noticed it like I do tonight. I can almost smell the fish, swimming out there in the black waters, all silvery-eyed and slippery.

Phil moves quickly, through the ER parking lot and out onto the sidewalk. He hardly has to push now: we're at the top of the hill, like I said, and it's an easy roll down to the main streets of the city. Well, maybe not so easy: Phil has to pull back on the handles of my chair so I don't, like, fly off by myself, sailing down the hill. Phil doesn't say a word until we're three blocks from the hospital, just at the top of the 700 block of Warren Street. Then he swerves me into the alley between a bank and some other place. He leans against a wall. "Got to have a smoke," he says and pulls a joint out of his pocket. He lights it up and takes a long, long pull. He holds it out to me. "Take a hit, Richard," he says. "You're on vacation."

I've got my pain patch on, so I'm already getting more dope than Uncle Phil can imagine, but hey—little more can't hurt. I take a hit, and it burns like hell and makes me dizzy. I hand it back to him and say, "Thanks, man. You relax. I'll stand watch." I roll myself out of the alley, just onto the sidewalk. I don't want to say so, but I don't like the dark in that alley—or the smell of cat piss. Anyway, I want to see the action.

Here's an okay thing about Hudson: the stores stay open for a couple hours in the early part of Halloween night so that the kids in the city can come around and trick or treat. They close three blocks—700, 600 and 500, that's it, because from 400 down, it's pretty dicey, neighborhood-wise—and no cars can come through. The little kids run around and have a ball. I did it myself, back when there were more real stores: Rogerson's Hardware, the Town Fair toy store, Sam's Market, all those good places. Now, it's very strange. All these New York City people came up and opened antique stores and art galleries and stuff. There're no *real* stores anymore—no food or toys or hammers and nails. Just places where me and Mom can't afford one single thing, and the owners know it the second we step inside, you can tell by their faces. More like museums than places to actually buy stuff. But this trend isn't so bad for Halloween. More than half those city people are gay couples, and they love this holiday—they dress up in crazy stuff and celebrate like mad. And candy? They give out great stuff. I'm talking *full-size* Hershey bars here.

Tonight, the place is jumping, I got to say. There's all kinds of music coming out of the shops, and there are guys in weird getups and masks dancing on the sidewalks. Little kids in those cheap costumes you get at the Dollar Store out on Fairview—one piece, cheesy nylon, masks held on by rubber bands. Power Rangers, Snow White, that kind of thing. Nothing even close to as cool as my werewolf costume. All the kids are running from store to store with shopping bags, taking in the loot. Mothers walk about half a block behind their kids, shouting at them to slow down, but not real worried because it's all such a mellow scene.

I'm sitting there, just grooving on the whole thing,

when this little girl, like around four, runs up and stares at me in my chair. She's got some kind of ballerina/fairy princess thing on—a purple fluffy skirt that's already in rags around her feet, a fake diamond thing on her head. She's a black kid with a million braids. She comes right on over and points at the wheelchair. Then she grabs on to one of the wheels. "This your costume, mister?" she says.

And I think about it. "Yeah," I say. "It is."

She tilts her head back and frowns. "What are you?"

"King of the cripples," I say. "My legs don't work. But I'm still king."

"You got no crutches. Where your crutches?" She looks at me hard, like I'm trying to fool her.

I'm thinking that one over when her mother—the youngest healthy woman I've seen in a while, really pretty, with a nice smile, smooth skin, and soft, round cheeks—runs up and grabs the little girl's hand. "Sorry," she says. She shakes her head. "She's out of control tonight. Too much sugar."

"No problem," I say.

The girl reaches into her shopping bag and drags out a bag of Skittles. "Here, mister cripple-man king with the no-good legs," she says. She drops the bag into my lap and then runs off, her mother following a few yards behind.

I open the bag and pour some Skittles into my hand. I toss them into my mouth, and that great sweet-sour, crunchy-chewy flavor just explodes in there. It's so good— it's like a rush of pure childhood. I can't stop eating them.

Phil comes out of the alley and laughs. "Hey, man. You scored some candy already? Fast mover." Then he grabs the bag out of my hand and empties the whole thing into his mouth.

I COULD HAVE STAYED on those three blocks all night, kids running around yelling and happy. But not Phil. I can see that he's getting bored after just pushing me around for about twenty minutes. I'm munching a Snickers when he says, "Okay, kid. Enough of this baby stuff. I got better plans for your Halloween than this."

And off we go. Like I said, Hudson is all downhill, right to the river. So Phil's really moving, and me, I'm rolling faster than I think, strictly, is safe. A couple times, Phil lets go of the handles and lets gravity take over. Then he trots along next to me, laughing. Once, I get going faster than he can run. That's scary, but also sort of amazing. I mean, the wind off the river is right in my face, and my mouth is, like, streaming full of real air. I hold on to my crown and I can feel that my cheeks are getting all red in that cold wind. Healthy, I think. I bet I look perfectly healthy.

I sort of want to just keep going, just take off and fly down to the river itself. But then, and I can picture this clear as day, I won't be able to stop, and this chair will carry me right into the water, wheels flashing and spinning. And the currents in the river, they're fierce. I spent my whole life listening to my mom go on and on about how I better not even think of fooling around down there, not even on the bank. She seemed to think that the river could reach out, like a big wet hand or something, and scoop me in. I'd go with the currents, all the way to New York City, and then out to sea. And she'd never see me again. I used to think about that, sitting on the windowsill at the end of the hall in the hospital in New York: I could see the river running right along the edge of the city, five times wider than it is up here, and I could imagine being in it, dead. A little speck of junk, moving on down. You'd think that would depress a kid in the hospital. Not so—it cheered me up, for some reason. Remember when that airplane landed in the Hudson, with all those people on the wings? I was there. I mean, I couldn't see it from my room, too far upstream, but we all kept crowding around the windows, pointing, thinking, Jeez, man, they were all okay, every one of them, saved. That pilot, he's a superhero. I kept thinking: saved. Those people were saved. Everyone got out alive. Every single one.

69

Anyway, I get scared of the rush of air in my face and the feeling that I can't stop and I reach down with both hands and jam on the brakes. It's still a few seconds before they really catch, and the whole chair kind of skids and slides, laying rubber out behind it. And that's way cool. People in the 200 block, where I land, are cheering, I swear. Laughing and pointing and cheering. Down here, where there's no more antique stores, only a whole lot of bars and a couple corner stores, people hang in the streets, and they like it when there's a little drama, I guess. A good fight. A crazy kid in a wheelchair, racing along like some kind of Evel Knievel knockoff in a cape and crown. I grin and take a little bow. But to tell the truth, all the candy I've just pounded down is up in my throat, and I'm pretty sure I'm going to puke.

Phil catches up and he sees that I'm kind of swallowing hard, and maybe I look a little green or something. Because he swings me into an alley and I hold my head over the side of the chair and bring it all up. Phil holds my cape out of the way and keeps my crown on my head. It's pretty messy, I got to say. All that good sweetness, turned sour and nasty, streaked with blood. Leaves a foul puddle on the ground, but that doesn't bother Phil a bit. He just backs up my chair and says, "Not to worry, Richard. People been tossing their cookies in this alley for centuries.

Archaeologists come along, they're going to find ancient bits of whale-blubber puke or something. Sailors from the olden days, Hudson was their favorite port town, you know? Famous for booze and whores and some very nice opium, I read somewhere. That's what the sailors found in Hudson."

He gets me back onto the street, heading for a bar three doors down. Funky sign over the door says FAT FRED FEATHERS and there's a picture of a dove or something landing on a fat man's shoulder. "Great," Phil says. "The old FFF is still around. Very cool." There's lots of loud music and people spilling out the door, some of them in masks and capes and all sorts of stuff. Women in sexy vampire makeup and fishnet stockings. One girl all dressed up in this pink gown, huge skirt and tight-laced top, boobs falling out the front, and a white-wigged head under her arm. Guy in full firefighter gear. Mad scene. "Hasn't changed a bit," Phil says. "Thank the Lord." And he starts to shout, "Make way, peasants. Make way for King Richard in his royal chariot, coming through. The king is thirsty, long live the king." The crowd laughs and they actually do make a big wide space, and my chair just fits through the doorway. Even the bouncer, huge dude in a Darth Vader mask, kind of shrugs and lets us through.

I have to admit, I've never been inside a bar. My mom

doesn't drink, and my high school friends and I, we just didn't come even close to looking old enough to stroll on in and order ourselves a beer. So this is a whole new experience, and it's making me kind of nervous. It's dark, for one thing. And it smells. Lots of hot sweaty people and lots of spilled beer, I'm guessing. What I once heard a Brit exchange student call a real pong. Always liked that word. People are about five deep at the bar and standing everywhere else. Lots in costume. A big green frog next to Osama bin Laden. Witch drinking with a nun. That kind of neat weirdness, all around. Everybody yelling above the music. So loud my head is pounding, and for a minute I feel like I'm going to puke again. But then the girl in the pink gown is bending down and my face is, like, right up against those breasts spilling out of that dress, and I can smell perfume instead of pong, and right away, I feel better.

Until she plunks a head into my lap. It's got red goop all over the neck and blue blank eyes, and its white wig is falling off. I take a deep breath. The girl is laughing. I don't want to seem dumb or wimpy or anything. So I poke my finger into one of the blue eyes and I say, cool as can be, "Marie Antoinette, I presume?"

And the girl puts both hands on her hips and then she dips down into a curtsy kind of bow, then wobbles back up. "*Mais oui*, my lord," she yells. "You really are royalty,

72

I can tell. None of the other bozos here got my costume. And I worked for days on it."

I look into her real face. It's round and plain, but she's got her hair all spiked up, dyed pink to match the dress, and she's wearing this necklace—a silver chain with a little miniature guillotine hanging down—and I've got to admire her creativity. And her chest. She's short and she's chubby and she's friendly and she seems sort of smart and she's talking to *me*? That about says it all.

Phil comes over, elbowing people out of his way. He's got two bottles of beer in his hands and he's grinning all over his face, looking at me and this sweet pink chick talking. He hands me one of the bottles—Blue Moon—and bows. "My liege," he says. "I leave you to your conquest." And then, with an even deeper bow, he hands the other bottle to the girl. "Mademoiselle," he says, "compliments of His Royal Highness."

She takes the bottle and curtsies at him. Then he disappears back into the crowd, backward, bowing all the way.

The bottle is dripping and cold. The label is very cool—a blue moon and a round orange pumpkin—and at first I just sit there like an idiot, holding it and looking at the moon. Then there's a clink and the girl in pink is saying, "Cheers, then," and she's tipping the bottle into her mouth.

So I do the same. It's so cold and nice on my raw throat that I just chug it. She's watching me, grinning, and so I've got to smile. "Thirsty work, being king," I say.

I don't know, maybe the beer plus the patch plus that one hit of Phil's joint, maybe all of that is a bit much. Or maybe my eyesight's more impaired than usual, by the mask and all. Because things get real fuzzy after I drink my first Blue Moon. There are others, too. Phil shows up every once in a while with another bottle and then bows his way out of sight. Last two times, he's got a pretty girl hanging off his side, arms around his waist. I think she's dressed as a leaf—can't remember why, I just picture leafiness in this haze.

The girl in pink—she says to just call her Marie—she sticks around. We talk—no clue about what—and laugh a lot. And at some point, she climbs into the chair with me, pushing her ass right into my lap. And I'm pretty sure I have a hard-on, although I'm kind of numb everywhere else. Because she giggles and kind of scooches herself around on there until there's a nice place for my hard-on to fit and she's moving her hips and humming a sweet little song in my ear. And then she whispers, "My lord, your willing servant would be most pleased to . . ." She licks my ear, all long and slow and wet. "If you'd like to step—um, roll—into my chamber."

74

I can't say a word, of course. I'm so dizzy and horny and, like, completely surprised that anyone, anyone at all, would offer to—whatever she's offering. So I just sort of grunt. But apparently, I've also got both hands on her breasts, so she takes that as a yes. She slides out of my lap—and, man, then I *know* I've got a major boner, cause ole Bingo is suddenly very cold and very lonely, sticking up into the air, until she sets the bloody head over it. She gets behind my chair and yells into the crowd, "Make way for the king. Make way, vassals." When people are a little slow to get out of our way, she just screams, "Move it."

Outside, the air is much colder, and I go to wrap my blanket-cape around my arms. But it's gone. Fell off somewhere. And for a second, I think of how Mom brought that blanket to every hospital, every single time, and it was always—always—waiting for me in my room after every torture and every operation, dark blue and starry and soft and warm and smelling like home, and I think I'm going to start to bawl. But then we're in, like, some sort of dark quiet place and Marie is kneeling in front of me.

"My sweet lord," she says. Then she takes the head off my lap and I manage to unzip my jeans and, whammo, my boy is right out there in the chilly air. It's looking sort of desperate, I got to say. And we both stare at it for a minute, and then she giggles and grabs it, and it's pretty obvious she hasn't got a clue what to do next, but she's trying and that's what counts. And there's a girl's hand on there and, really, that's all I need. I slide down and my head goes back against the back of the chair and I feel my crown drop away. Mask is still hanging on, though. Doesn't matter. Nothing matters except that she's still touching me, and then I'm, like, just shaking. Gasping. Moaning. She jumps back and loses her grip, and I think I'll die if she leaves me out there in the cold, but she doesn't: she leans in and holds me right between those round breasts. I must almost pass out, I swear, because next thing I know, she's standing up and wiping her chest with a Kleenex. Looking sort of surprised, but also kind of pleased with herself—and maybe with me. She smiles at me, anyway. I reach down and tuck my shriveled, happy little Bingo back into my jeans and zip up.

She rolls me out of the alley, and I'm a melted puddle of gratitude and can't say a thing—like my throat's been paralyzed. We hit the street and suddenly it's all noise and people pushing and yelling, and I don't know if she's taking me back to the bar or somewhere else, and I don't care because she can take me to hell itself at this point and I'll be happy. I just close my eyes and go with it.

Then we stop. I feel a hand on my shoulder. Not hers. Much too big and heavy to be hers. I open my eyes. We're in the light from the open doorway of the bar and there's someone leaning over me, breathing smoke and booze into my face. Holy shit. I've been caught by the devil himself.

"Well, well. What have we here?" Sylvie's father is standing over me, swaying and red-eyed and giving off heat like a chimney. He reaches down and tears my mask off. His spittle sprays onto my face. "Could it be? Our little wise-ass punk? Out of the hospital? Not so sick, after all? You lying fake."

I shake my head. "Just out on leave, sir," I croak out.

Marie bends over my head and tries to push the man's big hairy hand off my shoulder. "Leave him alone," she says.

He shifts his focus onto Marie, and I feel his hand tighten. "And who is this?" He breathes fire all over us and then he gives one horrible laugh that turns into a kind of sob. "Little bitch. Out here, your tits hanging out." He turns his eyes back to me. "You forget about my baby, Richard? You out here fucking around with whores while she—"

Marie's smack makes a bright red mark on his face. "Get out of our way," she says.

Sylvie's father grabs at her arm and she shrieks, and I make a grab for him, too, shoving both hands into his chest and pushing as hard as I can. But the man is immovable. He's crying and spraying spit everywhere and he's almost, I can hardly describe it, he's *howling*.

And then, I don't know, there's a million people coming

toward us, and Phil's in the lead. He leaps on Sylvie's father's back and they go down, and then I can't see a thing except for a whole bunch of feet and rolling backs. Marie pulls my chair out of the way and she sits down, hard, on the curb and sighs. "Nice friends you have," she says. And then she stands up and puts one hand on my head. Her hand runs along my bald scalp, feeling the bones of my skull. She bends down and looks, real close, at my eyes.

I can feel it, her staring. There's no mask now. And I know that I got no eyebrows and no eyelashes and that I look like a reptile. And I know she'll be completely disgusted and she'll never, ever put her mouth or her hands on me again.

Marie reaches down and touches one finger to my wrist. My hospital bracelet is right there, out of hiding. She's real quiet, and then she says, in this scared kind of voice I never want to hear again, "Jesus. Tell me it's not AIDS, okay? Just tell me that."

I want to close my eyes so I don't have to see her, but I can't. Got to meet people's eyes, Mom always says. Look 'em in the eye. So I look right at her, round face, pink hair falling down now, spikes all slumpy. "Not AIDS. Cancer. Not catching. No worries."

Doesn't matter, catching or not, she backs away. "Oh, man," she says. "I just . . ." She wipes her hand on her skirt.

And then she's gone. Running down the street, weaving between costumed people, her skirts pulled up and her strong legs churning.

***

Things blur. Sirens coming. Phil running, pushing my chair uphill, panting and grunting. Flashing lights. Phil turning, and we're in an alley and we're still moving fast, and then we're two blocks from Warren Street, on a quiet side street, and Phil parks me behind some bushes in somebody's front yard, and he leans over, holding his sides and groaning. "Shit," he breathes. "I am too old for this." He falls on his back onto the grass and lies there, his breath honking in his chest.

I feel strangely peaceful. I start to look around. This is a nice street; houses have pumpkins in their windows or on their porches. There's no trick-or-treaters left; it's late, I guess. Jeannette might be calling the police right now. Might have done it hours ago. I have no clue.

Phil's breathing calms down and he sits up. He's starting to laugh. "I hope you got some, Richard, me lad. Make it all worthwhile." His face is smeared with blood, and his knuckles are cracked wide open. He opens and closes his hand a few times, testing it.

"I sure did, man," I say. "Thanks."

He nods. "Mission accomplished." He sighs. "You want to go back there? That hospital? Or you want to go home? I can take you home, you know. We're, what? Five, six blocks away? From where you and Sisco live these days?"

I hear the real question in his voice and I get it: he doesn't know where we live. Mom doesn't want him to know. I close my eyes and I can picture it, the tiny little house Mom finally was able to buy us two years ago. He's right, it's only about five blocks away, to the north and west. Another quiet street, bitsy little ranch houses in bitsy little yards. But for Mom, it's a huge accomplishment, that house. It's huge. She *bought* it, fair and square, on her own. All by herself. My room is about eight feet by eight feet, hers not much more. But it's got a little lawn and a little porch, and she planted flowers, and there's a crab apple tree out back. It's our sanctuary, she said once. Our safe place. It's *ours*. Our house is something I think about a lot, sitting in my hospice room. Like how it's so close and how I could walk there anytime. Or take a cab. I could go home, lie around my room. But then Mom would have to take care of me, and I think that's way too hard, that this stuff should be left to the pros. Really.

And, anyway, Mom's sick. I bet she's in bed by now, wrapped in her old quilt and finally asleep after the trick-or-treaters. Last thing she needs? Phil and me, all messed up, knocking on her door.

"Hospital," I say. "Don't want to get Jeannette in trouble."

It is a long hard climb, uphill all the way. I'm too beat to help. It's all on Phil. And he manages, in short spurts with long rests. Give the man credit—he gets me back to Richie's World, almost safe and almost sound.

I WON'T EVEN TRY to describe the scene back at the hospital, it's so dark-edged and foggy in my head. I remember that the first thing I saw when Phil pushed my chair into the ER entrance and said good-bye, backing and bowing away, was the clock. It said 12:24. Not even Halloween anymore. Now it's All Souls' Day, I thought. I remember that. Or All Saints' Day. Whatever. I can't roll myself another inch. Can't get to an elevator, can't do one single thing. I just sit there. I might even be crying, I'm so tired. No, let's be honest: I *am* crying.

It all got kind of wild, I heard afterward, but at the time, I just drifted off to sleep. The ER staff, they read my bracelet and put me on a stretcher and got me back to the hospice unit. They understand the meaning of *No intervention*. Good people, those ER folks.

So I'm sent back to my floor where, Edward tells me

the next day, Jeannette was a complete and utter basket case, she was so scared. She was shaking and crying and she called him in early to take over her shift since she couldn't see straight. But, lucky thing, she didn't call the cops or my mother or anyone else, she was so afraid she'd lose her job. She just paced around, cursing the name of Philip Casey up and down the corridor.

Here we are, All Souls' or Saints' morning, and Edward's got his hand on my pulse and he's mad, I can feel it. I'm lying flat on my back and keeping my eyes closed, but I can feel heat in his hand. "She curse my name?" I ask.

"Same name, Mr. Casey. Same name." Edward drops my wrist and bends over, putting a hand on my chest. "You listen to me, Richie. You almost got a good nurse fired. You scared that poor woman to death. You can't do things like that. You . . ." Then he sighs. There's a long sort of pause, then he says, quiet, like he almost can't believe he's saying it, "You got to grow up, man."

And, you know, couple days ago, way back on Cabbage Night, I'd have laughed at that. But today, it makes a sort of sad sense. Might be something to think about, if I get a minute. But I can't think. All I can do is sleep. All day. I sense people walking in and out of the room, I hear them talking. I hear my phone ring, a lot. Finally, a nurse answers it and talks, low and calm, to my mom. Couple of times, I go to pull up my blue star blanket, I'm so cold. But it's not there. Somebody brings in a white hospital blanket and puts it over me. People stand around the bed, whispering.

But it's all part of a dream. I know that, because Marie is there, too. She's part of a crowd. A whole bunch of people I don't know, some of them in weird clothes, costumes maybe. Everybody's drinking, smiling. It's some kind of big party. Mom's there. She looks young and happy, and there's some guy with her, a guy I don't know, laughing and putting his hand on her neck. I know, in the dream, that I'm not born yet, that Mom hasn't got a care in the world. I'm not exactly me, not yet. I'm just, like, about to be. Hard to explain. I'm, like, there, watching, but I don't exist. Like I say, it's hard to explain.

I don't wake up, really, until it's dark outside. And when I do, it's Sylvie who's sitting next to my bed, all curled up on the lounge chair. I sit up, try to pull myself together. She's grinning. "Oh, man," she says. "You are so cool, Richie. You got out. You are, like, the hero of hospice. I even heard those two old men in 304 laughing about it. 'Kid got out,' they kept saying. 'Damned if he didn't.'"

I shake my head. I mean, here's a weird thing: I have never, ever been cool. Not even close. Never in my whole life. Ever.

Sylvie stands up, wobbly on her feet. I notice that she's dressed, wearing some kind of black top and jeans. They're about four sizes too big, but she's trying. She's got this funny little green striped hat on her head and she's wearing lipstick. She leans over my bed and puts her lips right next to my ear. "Richie," she says, clear as can be, "Richie, I don't want to be a virgin anymore. Okay?" She backs up. "Okay?"

I just stare at her.

She smiles. "You think about that. Okay? But not for too long." She walks out, holding on to the door frame with one hand, steadying herself, walking on her own. She's determined, anybody can see that.

Part II

NOVEMBER 1 – 3

So now it's night and I can't sleep. It's real quiet; the harpy's closed up shop for the day. Everyone else on the floor, I'm guessing, they're deep in sleep. But me, I'm sitting up in bed, kind of quivering with extreme wakefulness, my brain leaping. The excitement and surprise are just too much. I mean, I got a prospect that I never, ever saw coming: a girl—cool girl, pretty girl, popular girl—who wants me to be her first. As in, *FIRST*. My studly services have actually been solicited. I am not going to have to beg to even touch the girl, my usual MO. No, no, this time I have been formally invited. As in, Your Presence as Official Deflowerer Is Requested. (Bring Your Own Tool.)

Add this to the incontrovertible fact that just about twenty-four hours ago, I received my first—and please, please, please not last—blow job. Or something like it, anyway. Okay, so I'm inflating in my mind, big-time, I know that. Still, it happened, without one minute of pleading on my part. I mean, it was *offered*, man. Free and easy. Suddenly, I'm one hot dude. See, this is why it's cool to be alive, no matter what. It's all about surprises, the whole you-never-know thing, which really is turning out to be true. There is just no way in the whole wide world that I could have guessed, two days ago, that any of this was coming my way. What are the chances: seventeen-year-old virgin boy meets fifteen-year-old virgin girl in hospice, and they fall in love and/or lust, do the do—and meanwhile this ultrasexy boy gets his first bj, or whatever, on the side? Really, all of this in hospice where, believe me, this is not the norm. I mean, me and Sylvie, everybody, we're here because we got the Big Diagnosis: one month or less. You arrive and thirty days later, you either go home or Go Home. And yet. And yet, I am suddenly in full-swing, in-demand, hot-guy heaven. This does not compute, children. All I keep thinking, in my maturest mode, is Holy Shit!!!!!!!!!!!!!!!!!!!!!!

But just to make sure that all of this sudden uplift in my sex life doesn't make me forget that I do still have SUTHY Syndrome, I get to see Sylvie's father pacing the hall, making his umpteenth turn past my room. Never for a moment should I forget that Somebody Down Here hates me, too. Every time the man passes, he slows down and glares through the window in my door. His face is all dark and blotchy, bruised and cut, and it hangs there in the window like a bad moon rising, I swear. I close my eyes and feign sleep, but I can still feel his Evil Eye trained right on the center of my forehead. The beam of fury strikes like a bullet: *POW.* Finally, just before midnight, when the man has passed and repassed my room a million times, I can't take it anymore and I ring for a nurse.

It's poor old Edward, who's been pressed into doing, like, a triple shift. I mean, the dude looks so beat that I feel healthy in comparison. He's been bathing and lifting and medicating and who knows what all since seven A.M., taking the seven A.M. to three P.M. shift, then the three to eleven, and for some reason, is still here. His shoulders are bowed, I'm telling you, and his uniform is all wrinkled and stained with about eight best-left-unnamed substances. I feel sorry for bothering him, especially since he's still trying to be cheerful and reasonably professional even when it's clear that's a huge stretch of human patience. "What's up, young Richard?" he asks.

"Nothing much," I say. "I'm feeling better, actually. I just need help getting out of bed, okay? Can't sleep. Can I hang with you guys for a while?" They let me sit at the nurses' station some nights, when things are quiet. There's some laughing there, usually, and some fat-full, salt-heavy, sugar-laden, unhealthy snacks for those who choose to eat. Some company for the sleepless, at least. Nurses, they get the middle-of-the-night blues, too. How could they not?

"Oh, sure, like you deserve privileges." His eyebrows pull together. Then he sighs. "Okay, fine. We could use some cheering up." He grabs my chair and hoists me into it.

I shouldn't ask. Should never ask around here. But I can't help it. "Who?"

Edward steers the wheelchair so I can see into room 304, the room that the two ancient dudes share—well, shared. Past tense. The bed by the window is all neatly made up, empty. The curtains are pulled around the other one.

"Oh, no," I say. "Did one of those guys actually *die* while the other one was right there in the room? I mean, isn't that against regulations?" I mean, really. Usually they hustle the actually—as in right-now, today, this minute—dying folks into private rooms for family privacy and to prevent roommate trauma. The least they can do, don't you think? Give everybody some breathing space for those last breaths.

He gives a snort. "Let's just say it's frowned upon. But sometimes, we don't know. Thought the man was taking a longish sort of nap, but got busy. Missed what was happening, like a total fool."

At the nurses' station, I can see that everyone's down.

They're all just subdued. There's a Br'er there and two aides, along with Edward and me and a nurse I don't know. She's the kind that wears a stiff white cap bobby-pinned to her hair, and the white cap has one of those black velvet ribbons running across it. That kind of cap always spells trouble, in my experience. The cap sits on top of a helmet of gray hair. She's got *supervisor* and *reports* written all over her. She looks at me hard, like I'm some strange beast and she's pissed off that I've escaped from my cage, but then she glances at Edward's tired face and doesn't say anything, just makes a *tsk*ing sound with her tongue. I can tell that this group is going to bring me down from my sex-happy high, big-time. "Going for a drive, daddio," I say to Edward. "Don't wait up." I wheel myself off down the hall.

First stop, Sylvie's room. If I can see in, maybe I'll know that her father's given up prowling and has crashed on his little cot. Or gone off to drink in a local bar, like he always seems to do once Sylvie's asleep. I ease up to the doorway, hands on wheels, ready for a quick reverse should the man be in there, like some grizzly bear in his cave, protecting his young. The door's open, and I lean in. The cot is empty. There's a big half-moon hanging outside one of the windows. I roll farther in, quiet as a paraplegic mouse. I park myself just at the foot of Sylvie's bed.

The room smells girly-sweet. There's a big bunch of

pink roses in a vase by the bed. The little night-light over her bed is on—it's never really dark around here. I can see the shape of Sylvie in the bed, curled on her side under a sheet. I focus on the curve of what I assume is her hip and get a big lump in my throat. I know, I know: a big lump in my crotch would be more promising. But that's not happening at the moment. I'm not sure it ever will with Sylvie. Partly because she's sick, partly because she's fierce. Partly because her old man would fry my ass. But mostly because I got this deep sense that she is so far out of my league that I'm dreaming if I think my lips might ever touch hers. Like they wouldn't even match, you know? Her private-school, smart-girl, good-family, college-prep lips are just not the same shape as mine. Like we're different species. I roll over to the bulletin board and check out, in the iffy moon/ hospital light, all the pictures her mother has put there, like I got to make sure, like maybe she wasn't so gorgeous and perfect back in her other life.

But she was. It's all there, the evidence. Pre-SUTHY, this girl was seventeen million notches above me on the social scale. At least. Hell, she was way ahead of me on the whole evolutionary scale. Like I'm some sort of slump-backed ape-creature and she's the tall straight human, already using her thumbs to make fire and wheels. I keep looking and looking, though, searching the eyes and the body and the hair and the skin in the pictures. Like maybe, even then, there was some sort of sign on her. Like a stain or something. Something to show that she was marked. Some warning that at fifteen, she'd end up here, with the likes of me. And if I could find it, then I'd be able to match my sorry self to hers. I don't know, something like that, that's what I'm searching for. I roll over to the bunch of roses, wanting a good long smell of their sweetness. There's a little white card tucked into the vase. I pluck it out and read, *Baby, I miss you. Get better, okay?* It's signed *Chad.* Wouldn't you just figure her boyfriend would be named Chad? I mean, come on. I haven't got a shot. I put the card back and decide to just roll myself out of there, quiet and simple. Have some dignity, man, I tell myself.

"Hey." Her voice raises the hair on the back of my neck, it's so sweet and low.

I swing my chair around and look at her. She hasn't moved, still curled on her side. But her eyes are open and they shine in this little patch of moonlight that's broken into her room. It's amazing—how beautiful she looks, right then. There's this little haze of dark hair growing on her head, soft and fuzzy. Her eyes are dark as night and huge in her thin, white face. "Hey," I say.

She crooks a finger through the bars of her bed, bringing me closer. "Dad's gone?" It's a question.

"Yeah. I think so." I roll closer and put my hand around one of the steel bars. It's shining in the moonlight, all silver.

She smiles, a flash of white teeth. "Yeah, well. Don't count on it. He'll be back. He takes long walks, he says. Comes back reeking of bourbon. Whatever." She reaches out and pulls my hand through the bars, curling her fingers around mine and then putting both of our hands under her sheet, against her belly. She's wearing some kind of long, loose tank top thing. And I'm pretty sure that's all she's wearing. "Well, then. Let's carpe diem, dude."

I can feel my heart thunking against my ribs. And I can feel her heart beating against her ribs. It's the coolest thing: they're in sync, those two hearts. And the skin on her belly is smooth as silk. I rub my rough knuckles against it, up and down. She guides our hands a little and makes them run over a bumpy line that cuts her in half, going north and south, sternum to, I assume, crotch.

"Scar," she whispers. "Ugly as hell. Like some hideous railroad track."

I shake my head, trying to think of something gallant and comforting to say. I can't. I let go of her hand and take one finger of my own, running it along the scar, up and down. Up, it starts between two tiny breasts. Down, it ends where hair might start, if she had hair. I stop there. Finally, my voice opens up. It sounds all cracked and funny, but at least I can form words. "Ugly, hell," I say. "It's the stairway to heaven." There it is, I realize—the thing that puts her on my level. Or me on hers. Or something. I move my finger one squinch lower.

She makes a little sound, just a soft intake of breath, and rolls onto her back. She catches my hand and holds it to her. Then she presses it even lower and lets go. She giggles. "No need for bikini wax," she says. "All taken care of by Dr. Chemo." She lifts her hips, just a smidge, and her eyes close. "Go for it, Rich-Man," she says.

And, you know, I would, I really would, except I want so bad to kiss her first. Like I can't just grab the girl's privates, can I, without some kind of prelude? I just can't. My mama raised a gentleman. I roll as close as I can get to her bed and try to lean in over the bars. It's almost impossible, though, unless you're a giraffe. It's awkward as hell.

She notices that my hand isn't progressing, I guess, and she opens her eyes. She sees me looming over her, halfway out of my chair and halfway in. She snorts out a laugh. "Oh, Richard," she says. "I'm such an ass. Sorry." She pushes the button that lowers the side of the bed.

I stand up; I'm not really wheelchair-bound, after all. Just a little shaky in the legs. Well, a lot shaky, it turns out.

97

I fall on top of her, and all of a sudden we're both giggling like maniacs, our legs all knees and ankles, knocking into each other, and our elbows in each other's faces.

She's better at this than I am, I have to say. Without doing much, she kind of slides under me and then we're lying chest to chest, crotch to crotch. I take a breath as she runs one hand along my chest. Then she gives a little shriek. "Oh my god. You've got one, too," she says. Her small fingers play up and down what the docs call my midline incision. Been opened and zipped back up six, seven times. Her hand is cool, and I, like, just freeze as it creeps lower and lower to where hair should be and isn't. "Oh, man," she says, "we match! Except for this." And, no shrinking violet she, she just goes on ahead and grabs, while I lower my face and find her mouth with mine.

And that's exactly how we are when Edward bursts into the room and flicks on the overhead light. Then we're blinded.

I try to pull the sheet over us. "What?" I say. "What?"

Edward is whispering, loud. "Come on, you two. Move it. Her father's back."

I will not dignify my exit from the room with a description. It's too embarrassing. Let's just say I was bundled like a baby into the wheelchair and pushed at amazing speed by Edward into the room next door. From which Edward and I peeped out like scared rabbits while Sylvie's dad wobbled down the hallway, muttering and growling to himself. He peeked into Sylvie's room, where I presume she had the smarts to look like a sleeping innocent, then he kept going, making one more lap around the hallway.

As we watch the man's back recede, it takes me a minute to realize that we're in 304, the room with the recently vacated bed. I can tell that Edward is about ready to punch my lights out, and he's opening his mouth to start some big-time lecture when I hear something: a weird kind of humming noise. "Hey," I whisper to Edward. "Shut up. Listen." Maybe the bed itself is moaning? Maybe it's haunted? I mean, I don't believe in ghosts, not much, but I do kind of think a guy might hang around, some way or another, for a couple hours after he stops breathing. Only makes sense, right? Not like some otherworldly presence or anything, just like the guy he was. So I try to remember the old man who lived in it, the guy who liked soccer, guy who laughed, I heard, at my Halloween escape. But then I can hear the sound more clearly and I can tell it's not coming from his bed after all.

It's coming from behind the curtains of the other bed, a kind of mumbling snuffle. Then humming again. A melody. *Dum de dum, dum de dum.*

"God almighty. Taps," Edward says on one long sigh. "That's taps."

Of course it is: *Day is done. Gone the sun.* I can hear it perfectly now. And it's, like, completely unbearable. Saddest sound on earth. I roll over and pull back the curtain. This is entirely against hospice etiquette, I realize. But, hey, it's been a strange night, right? And this guy can probably still smell the Grim Reaper's aftershave and he's humming taps, and I figure he could use a little company. "Sir? You okay in here?" I ask.

He's sitting straight up in bed, his right hand over his right eye, bony elbow out at a sharp angle. It takes me a minute to get that he's not holding his head in pain or something. No. He's saluting. The man is sitting up in his bed, straight as a board, hospital gown crumpled around his neck, skinny legs hanging off the side, saluting. He drops his hand when he sees me. "The man was a soldier," he says. "Survived Bataan, damn it."

Well, what are you gonna say? I nod. "Yes, sir," I croak out. I kind of want to salute, too—it would feel right. But I'm no soldier, and I haven't earned that. I'm just a kid. So I just repeat, "Yes, sir."

He leans forward. "Want to play some gin rummy, kid?"

Edward sits down on the empty bed and starts to laugh. At least that's what I think he's doing. He's making laughlike noises, anyway, even though he keeps wiping his hands down his face.

And that's how, somehow, five guys start playing cards in room 304. Gin isn't really my game, I got to say. Poker, now that's what I like. But, hey, the old guy gets to choose, right? It's his room, after all. So gin it is. There's four of us ranged around a bed table on plastic chairs, the old guy in his bed, propped on pillows. Me, the old guy, Mrs. Elkins's son, Edward, and—heaven help my sorry ass—Sylvie's dad, we all got in on it. Don't know how, exactly, we all ended up there, but Edward said he was too tired to go home, and Mrs. Elkins's son said if he didn't get out of his mother's room he was going to lose his mind, and, well, Sylvie's dad just showed up, wearing a suit that looked like it had been on him for three or four weeks and smelling like booze and smoke, eyes two red slits in a puffy bruise-splotched face. And that man came to play, I'll say. Showed no mercy, I'll tell you. I mean, I expected that he'd want to beat my sorry ass into the ground, even if he didn't know exactly what I'd been—almost—up to with his little girl. Okay, that's fair. He could whip my butt and I'd call it even. Fair's fair.

But the man doesn't even have the basic decency to let the old guy win a hand. Nope. Just wipes the floor with all of us, cackling like a hyena every time he shouts "Gin." Which he does, like, incessantly, even when he hasn't really got it. It's the most annoying thing you can imagine.

I get to shout "Gin" only once, and when I do, I'm sorry I ever made a sound. His eyes burn holes in my chest, sweartogod.

He takes every hand, other than that one I squeak in. Drinks all the green minicans of ginger ale and eats all the little packages of saltines, too. Prick.

Game goes on until the white-capped nurse, lips pressed shut, comes in and says, "Gentlemen. Desist. You are disturbing the other patients."

I look up, surprised to see sunlight coming in the window. Square patches of light on the yellow walls. Morning. All Souls' Day over. Halloween over. Cabbage Night over. So it's already, what, November 2? Man, only ten days until my birthday. And I got things to do.

For the first time in weeks, I'm hungry. Got to build up my strength if I'm going to be able to do my duty to Sylvie—and maybe other desperate women? I roll back to my room, and when they bring the breakfast tray I swallow big mouthfuls of slimy egg. Two pieces of toast. Orange juice. Oatmeal. And then I take a long nap.

AND WAKE UP SO freaking sick that I can barely reach
the puke basin in time. I retch for, like, twenty minutes,
and then my guts knot and I know I got to get to the bathroom real quick. So I stagger my way out of bed and sit in
there for what seems like an hour, sweat pouring out of my
skin and pure liquid out of my butt. Finally, I'm so dizzy
that I have to press the red emergency button on the bathroom wall. Cannot pass out, I say to myself while I wait.
There are black smudges in my vision, with bright lights
popping out around them. Will not pass out. Passing out
is not an option.

I manage to maintain consciousness, but just. Insult
to injury: the nurse that comes in is the white-capped one.
She's all clean and starchy, even if she has been here all
night and half the day. She takes one look at my crumpled,

sorry self slumped on the toilet and—I got to give her some credit here—she says not one word. No lecture, no *tsk*ing, no nothing. She just gets cool washcloths on my face and neck. And she helps me up and into the lounge chair in my room, pulling curtains around me. She whips off my T-shirt and sweatpants with, like, only three moves. She washes all of me—and I mean *all,* with not a peep out of Bingo—with warm, soapy cloths. She dries all of me with a scratchy towel and throws my arms into a clean hospital gown. She's got an aide making up the bed clean and she's got me in it in another three moves and she's putting Puke-Away on my wrist. Okay, the woman is good at the mechanics of her job, I admit. But not exactly comforting. She manages all of this bathing without unpursing her lips once, I swear. A master of control. Without saying a word, she scares me to death.

Finally, when I'm tucked in like a three-year-old, side rails up, she speaks: "You will not get out of bed again today, young man. You will bother no one on this floor. Understood?"

I nod. "Yes, sir, ma'am."

For the first time—maybe the first time ever—she smiles. Like a shark. "My name is Mrs. Jacobs, Richard. I raised three boys of my own. Teenage boys hold no terrors for me."

I choke down what I want to say: *So, are those three boys still in therapy?* What I do say isn't so funny, but I figure it'll make her feel lousy, and I say it loud: "So, Mrs. Jacobs. Yeah, I guess you are an expert then. But, hey, any of those three boys end up in hospice?"

Her face gets very still. Then her eyes get wet. "No," she says, so soft I have to lean forward to hear her. "My youngest died in a car crash. He was fourteen. He never made it to hospice." And she walks out of the room.

"So," I say to myself, sinking down into the clean sheets, "ever feel more like a complete and absolute shit, Richard?"

"No, sir," I answer. "No, sir."

***

And that state of affairs, that feeling like shit on a brick, gets even worse. I'm just sitting there, looking out into what seems like the darkest November day on record, huge gray clouds low and wet in the sky, when my mom calls. Somehow or other, she's heard about my Halloween outbreak, and she is, let us say, a bit upset. She coughs between every phrase and she's sort of choking and yelling all at once. "That miserable, sneaking Phil," she keeps saying. "I can't believe you went with him, Richard. You went *out*. I cannot believe it. He's *always* been trouble. You know that. He is *trouble*. And you listened to him? You went *outside* with him?"

I know enough to keep quiet while the ranting goes on, and then I say, "Ma, you don't sound so good. Nasty cough. How are you?"

And then she just starts to bawl. "My fever's up again," she wails. "And the tests were positive—it's the real flu, some kind of nasty strain. I can't come see you. Oh, Richie, they won't let me in. I begged and begged your doctors, said I'd wear a mask. I even called the CEO of the hospital. I said I'd wear a hazmat suit. They still won't let me onto your floor. Said if I came, security would escort me out. I can't stand it. I can't stand it." Then she's just sobbing—no words, only wet gulps.

Listening to her, my chest feels like it's crushed under a load of stones and someone keeps heaping them on. Every sob, another boulder. "Ma," I keep saying. "It's all right, Ma. I'm fine, I swear. Come on, Ma. Don't cry. Stop crying." My own voice breaks, and then, of course, I'm crying like a baby, too. And then I can't breathe and I think maybe I'll die, right here right now. And that would be kind of a relief.

But I don't.

So we both sit there, on opposite ends of the phone, crying until we can't cry anymore. We both get quiet, clinging to our separate phones. Then, finally, I have an idea. "Call Grandma," I wheeze. "I want Grandma to come up and take care of you. It's time. Do it."

There's a very long silence. See, my mom and her mom don't see eye to eye on much of anything. Not since my mom was seventeen and knocked up and wouldn't even tell anyone who did that to her. Locked her lips. Or maybe even since way before that; maybe from when Grandma, a tough Jersey girl, was sixteen and herself knocked up, and the baby in her belly—the one that made her leave high school and miss her prom and basically ruined her life—was my mom. I mean, it's hard to understand, for me. They talk on the phone, like, daily, but in person, they're horrible. In person, they're crazy, always mad, always both of them right, about everything. Both of them just constantly pissed off and throwing verbal punches. But from what I can hear, when Mom's whispering on the phone lately, Grandma has been begging to come up, to help us, she keeps saying. For months, she's been begging. To be here, to see us through this. But Mom's been saying nothing but no. No. No. Not yet. Like she's totally terrified that when she calls her mom and lets her come up here, that's like the signal for the end. Surrender. White flag. SUTHY wins. And maybe even Grandma feels like that, too, because she hasn't just shown up on her own, either.

I get it, I really do, but right now I just want my mom not to be alone. I want someone to take care of *her,* for once in her life. 'Cause if she's all alone and she's sick and crying, I swear to god, I'll break out of here and take care of her myself. I'll call a cab. I'll walk.

And that's what I tell her. "Ma, do it. Or I'll come home. I'll just fucking break out of here and come home. I mean it. No one can stop me, if I really want to go. You know what? Maybe I'll just call Phil. He'll come get me."

There's still silence. See, here's the other thing: she's totally scared that if I step one inch outside of this hospital, germs will pile all over me and carry me off. That's part of why she's so pissed at Phil. He took me outside these sacred walls. She thinks—she makes herself think—that being in a hospital keeps me safe. Maybe even that a hospital, despite all she knows about it, equals a cure. The miracle around the corner.

"I mean it, Ma. I'm on my way." I throw off my sheets and start banging the rails of my bed, loud enough for her to hear me.

Finally, there's just the smallest whisper. "Okay," she says. "Okay."

And what scares the holy shit out of me is her voice, giving in. Giving up.

* * *

Rest of the day, I lie on my side in bed, looking out into the gray sky. I keep my back to the door. If anyone comes by, they'll think I'm asleep. Once, I think I smell Sylvie's perfume, floating in from the doorway, and I hear a soft little, "Hey, Rich-Man," but not even that can make me turn around.

Three o'clock rolls around and Edward comes in. He bends over the bed and says, "You still with us, my man? I heard you had a rough morning."

I just sort of shrug under the sheet.

He puts a hand on my shoulder. "Sulking, Richard? That's not like you."

I roll over and glare into his round face. "I just wanted to eat, man," I say. "I wanted to, you know, get stronger. And all it did was make me puke my guts out."

He nods. "Right. I get it. You want to eat, good. Just don't be a total jerk about it. Think, man. You can't just start scarfing down everything in sight, out of nowhere, after so long. Got to start small. Jell-O. Soup. Apple juice. Ginger ale."

I think about it. "Sylvie's dad drank all the ginger ale. Every single can from the whole freaking fridge. Prick."

Edward laughs. "Richard, there is an endless and everlasting supply of ginger ale around here, trust me. So sit yourself up and I'll bring you some."

I elbow my way into a sitting position. "The Big Nurse said I can't get out of bed."

He packs pillows behind my back. "Mrs. Jacobs went home early," he says, all low-key and no-blame. Then he whacks me upside the head. Gentle, but still, a substantial whack. "She's a good nurse, Richard," he says. "A really, really good nurse. And she's had a rough time, and you go and remind her of it. Everybody's got troubles, you know that? The world's a universally sad and fucked-up place. People hurt, all of them. You beginning to get that? Or do you still think it's just you, man? Only you that suffers? Like you've been singled out?" He doesn't wait for an answer, just heads out the door. Then sticks his head back in. "I forgot. You got a visitor. Been waiting a while for you to wake up. You up to it?"

I look up. "A visitor? Who?"

He winks and waggles his eyebrows. "An interesting girl, young Richard. My, my, my. You are turning into quite the rock star."

I sit up straighter, and before I can think how to get out of the dorky gown—this one has cowboys on it, like it escaped from pediatrics—and into a T-shirt, this *interesting* girl sticks her head inside the room. She's got black, black hair—like she dipped it in tar and spiked it up in points—and black eyeliner an inch thick. She's wearing camouflage pants with a bright orange vest. It's like she's copied her outfit from *Field & Stream*. Like she's just stopped by on her way to the woods, got her rifle in the pickup, got doe pee sprayed on her neck. I haven't a clue who this is, but what the hey? I try to be charming anyway—because it is a female of the species, after all. "Hey," I say. "Got your buck yet?"

She blinks those black-lined eyes. "What?"

I point toward her vest. "It's deer season. Started yesterday. And you're wearing . . ." I can see that she hasn't got a clue what I'm talking about and she's ready to back right out of the room, so I give up on being clever. "Never mind."

She hovers in the doorway and then holds out a shopping bag. "Your cape, Your Majesty, washed and all." She makes a little awkward bow.

I get it, finally. "Marie! You look so different. Hey, come on in."

She smiles then and walks over to the bed. She shakes the bag and out falls my starry night blanket.

I sweep it up and try to cover up the fact that I'm ready to cry at the sight of it. I hold it to my nose. "Smells nice," I say. It does—all clean and fresh. "Thanks." I swing it up around my shoulders like a cape again. "Have a seat." I wave, regally I hope, toward the chair next to my bed.

111

"It was all crumpled up in the bar," she says. "I had to look for a while. I took it to the Laundromat, used fabric softener and all." She puts a hand on the bed rail. "Listen. I want to say I'm sorry. I kind of freaked, you know, when I heard you were sick. I thought—well, it doesn't matter what. I'm sorry."

I take a minute to really look at her. Under the hostile hair and aggressive eyeliner, there's a chubby, young, shy kind of face. And round blue eyes. Her fingernails are chewed to ragged stubs. I put my hand over hers. "You were great," I say. "You were super."

Her face lights up. "Really? You're not, like, mad? Or anything?"

"Or nothing, Marie."

She leans forward. "My real name is Kelly," she says. "Marie was just part of my costume. Marie was, like, you know, my alter ego? Like, I could be much braver, more, uh, bold as Marie than as me? Mostly, you know, I'm kind of, I don't know, scared and not too smart. A real dim bulb, my brother says. Do you understand that, how a costume, you know, can make a huge difference?"

I'd like to say that I'm paying full attention to these deeply insightful questions about issues of human identity and all—but, really, I am looking down her vest. See, she isn't wearing a shirt under it, even. I mean, it's just a shiny orange vest with a deep V open in front and kind of wide-open sides, and from any angle, there are big-time, fully visible breasts under there. Creamy plump round white breasts, rolling around free. And hazy memory or not, I can most definitely remember sliding between those breasts. I try to pry my eyes upward, focus on the girl's face. But once I do, I see that she's holding her bottom lip between her teeth. And I most surely do remember those lips, too. And I can feel myself making a tent pole beneath the sheets. "Yeah," I say, brilliantly. "Well, nice to meet you, Kelly-Marie."

She giggles. "And, you, too, Richard Casey." She leans even farther and the breasts press right up against the bed rail and kind of squoosh over the top. "See? I had to find out your real name, too. I kept asking around. Some people knew your uncle and some know your mom, too, and they told me the story about you—how you've been sick for a long time and how you were here and, well, I found you, didn't I?"

I'm resisting, just barely, the urge to grab her and haul her into the bed, when Edward comes in. He smiles this great big grin and nods at Kelly-Marie. "Hello," he says. "Thought you guys might like something to drink." And in his hands there are two cold cans of Coke. Not the hospice-size minicans. Not ginger ale. Real Cokes.

113

And I know that he must have gone to one of the machines down on the first floor, by the ER, and actually bought these himself. Shelled out a buck fifty each. Sometimes, you know, human kindness just knocks you off your feet. "Thanks, man," I say. I hope he can hear how I know what he did and how I really appreciate it.

He waves a hand and takes off, swinging the door almost all the way closed on his way out.

So that Kelly-Marie and I can sit there and drink our Cokes and talk and laugh and flirt. Just like any other teenagers, anywhere in the whole wide world.

IT'S GOING FINE — TURNS OUT Kelly-Marie is a freshman at Hudson High and she's heard of me because I'm a senior — or I would be if I ever went to school. And I'm sort of famous, in a lousy way: the boy that's always sick. She doesn't say it, so I do: "Yep, that's me. The Incredible Dying Boy." And then I feel like a real jerk because her blue eyes get so sad. I laugh. "Not really," I say, trying not to sound totally lame.

She brightens up. "Really? You're not?"

I look at her and I say the stuff I usually say to my mom when she's down. "Hell, no. Listen, right now, right this minute, there's a whole bunch of science geeks, right? I mean, like, all of these super-smart research dudes, and they're working away like madmen, day and night and fucking day again. I mean, these guys, they're at Harvard and MIT and Columbia and shit. And they're up to their asses in test tubes and gene therapies and all kinds of secret stuff. They're on it, believe me. Coming up with the cure. I totally trust those guys. We expect a breakthrough any day now." In my head, to myself, I go, Yeah, right. But she's buying it, I can tell. Just like my mom does; people believe what they want to believe, I guess.

Kelly-Marie is nodding, smiling. I'm feeling better that I made her feel better. Then the door swings open and there's this skinny, fuzz-headed, brown-eyed girl standing there: Sylvie. Wearing a black tank top and black—I don't know what you call them, like leggings or tights or something, with her feet bare. She's just, like, hovering there, all in black, like the Ghost of Christmas Yet to Come, you know? She's got this scary smile on her face, and I notice how she inherited her father's sharp teeth. "Yeah," she says, all cool and snarky. "Those science guys, they're working on it, for sure. No doubt they'll figure it all out, in, say, another couple of years. May be just a tad late for us, but what the hell. I'm sure *somebody* will be cured. That's what counts. The good of the human race. Not some puny little individuals. Right, Richard?"

Sylvie walks into the room—walks, mind you. And she's pretty steady, too. She's not even holding on to anything, that's how determined—and mad, I think—she is. She goes right over to Kelly-Marie and looks her over, sort

116

of like she's a pile of dog shit someone left on the carpet. "Hey," she says. She holds out a bony white hand. She's completely elegant and looks like that actress in the old movies. Audrey Hepburn, that's it, in the movie where she's the princess trying to be normal. Except Sylvie's totally in control, directing the whole scene. "I'm Sylvia," she says. "Richard's girlfriend."

Kelly-Marie kind of slumps. Suddenly, she's just plain Kelly, a fat freshman girl in a weird outfit, trying way too hard to look cool. She stands up and takes hold of Sylvie's hand for one millisecond. "Hey," she says. "I—um—just came over to return Richard's blanket." She gestures toward my starry cape. "I'm going now." And she scoots out of the room, slamming the door behind her.

Sylvie stands there with her hands on her hips, glaring first at the door, then at me. "So. How'd you misplace your precious blankie, Richard? Would you care to explain that to me?"

"Not sure," I say. And, really, I'm not sure, right? I mean, there are a few possibilities, like when Kelly-Marie was touching me or when . . . I think it wisest not to mention the possibilities. "Sometime Halloween night."

"You were with that girl Halloween night? That stupid fat, trashy, pathetic wannabe Goth?"

I should defend Kelly-Marie. I really should. Because

she's a nice girl, kind and generous. With great breasts. But I'm withering under the heat of Sylvie's eyes. "I wasn't *with* her with her. Just a girl I met at a bar." That sounds, I have to admit, sort of cool actually, so I take it one bit further. "She was dressed as Marie Antoinette. Really creative costume. Carrying her head."

"Uh-huh. I'm sure her costume was an absolute scream." Sylvie presses the button to slide my bed rails down and then she slithers in next to me. She throws one leg over my hips and moves one hand across my belly. She whispers into my ear, lips touching my skin. "Carrying her head, huh? And giving head, too, I imagine. Right?"

"Um. I really can't reveal—"

"Bullshit," she says. Those cool, thin fingers reach my crotch and her tongue circles my ear. "You know what? There's something very attractive about a sexually experienced man, Richard. Very much a turn-on. And, as it happens, my mom and the boys went home early this afternoon; one of the twins is sick. And my dad's coming in late. So. . . ." Her fingers start to stroke.

I think I might die right then and there, happy, with her hand moving on me. I think I might skip right over death and go straight to heaven. The hand moves faster, and Sylvie's teeth close on my earlobe. And then, sooner than I'd like to admit, I do go to heaven, or something like it, right there in my cowboy nightgown. Yippee ki o, ki ay.

For the first time in my life, I get to experience afterglow. Sylvie's all curled up and I'm rubbing her back, slipping my hand under her shirt, pulling it up around her neck and cupping her breasts in my hands. Her butt is pressed right up against me. I got to say that I'm feeling so tired that it's hard to just be there, in the moment, you know? Like, I want so much to *be here,* knowing that I've got my hands on a girl's breasts, like this is something I have to take in, just totally absorb, so it'll be a sweet memory forever. But I'm fading. In and out. And I think Sylvie is, too, she's so quiet. But her breathing, it's raspy and quick. I can feel every breath she takes, her little ribs like sticks under my fingers, barely moving up and down. I can feel every bone in her back, too, sharp against my chest. I tuck my head over hers and feel myself letting go, sliding into sleep. But she turns over all of a sudden and jostles me awake. She lies on her side and scoots up on the pillows so we're eye to eye. I notice that her eyelashes and eyebrows are just starting to come back, soft black bits of haze. Her eyes are really bright.

"Are you scared, Richard?" she asks.

I want to look away. I feel my eyes move away from hers. "Of your dad? Shit, yes."

She grabs my face with both hands. "Look at me," she says, her voice rough. "And don't be an ass. I asked you a real question and I want a real answer. Are you afraid, Richard?"

I look into her eyes. They look hot, like two coals. Maybe she's got a fever. More like she *is* a fever. "Okay, yeah," I say. "I'm scared to death." I try to chuckle on the last word, show her it's a kind of sick joke, but I can't. I feel my own eyes get wet. Serious she wants, serious she gets. "Yes, Sylvia," I say. "I am most definitely scared."

She nods and lets go of my face. "I thought so." She scootches back a bit and turns on her back, putting her hands under her head. "Well, I'm not."

I lean up on an elbow, looking down at her. "No? Really? Come on, you got to be serious, too, Sylvia. I was."

She smiles. "It's true. I'm not scared, Richard. Because it's not going to happen, not yet. I'm going to get better." She closes her eyes and her voice gets sleepy, but she keeps going. "Not because of some scientific miracle, either. Just because I will not allow it. It is not acceptable." There's a long sigh, and then she's sound asleep.

For a while, I stay there, just looking at her face. With her eyes closed, all the life goes out of it. All the fierceness disappears, and what's left is the tiniest, most fragile little face you ever saw. You can see the skull under her skin, her jawbone and the dips of her temples, deep blue. Her skin is dry, like thin paper. She hasn't got the strength, I think. She's just too little. I put both my arms around her and wrap her up in my legs. I try to make a cave for her, like I can keep her totally protected somehow. I pull her in and fall asleep.

* * *

Sometime, who knows how long later, the lights in the room blast on and grab me out of sleep. I look up, all blind and confused. And Br'er Bertrand steps in. "Richard," he booms, in his heartiest Br'er voice, "I've got something for you."

Now, I'd like to say, for the record, that Sylvie is so tiny that she could have simply remained still and silent under the sheet and probably been invisible. She really could have. We could have gotten away with it, totally. But you got to know by now that discretion is not one of Sylvie's strong points. No indeed. Sylvie is what my grandma calls a pisser. So the girl sits straight up, tosses off the sheet and stretches her arms over her head, letting her naked breasts point toward the sky. Between them, there's that huge railroad track scar, all exposed, red and shiny in the bright light. And she does not seem to give a shit. Slowly, she pulls her tank top into place and then, slowly,

slowly, slowly, swings her legs over the side of the bed. She smiles at the Br'er and says, "Good evening. Richard and I were just celebrating evensong. We like to join in prayer, every evening. Really, really join. The couple that prays together, stays together." She walks out of the room like a tiny queen, hips swinging.

To say that the good Br'er is speechless is like saying the Grand Canyon is a hole in the ground. The man's jaw actually falls to his chest, and he sits down, hard, on the bedside chair.

I sit up, tuck my rumpled and still-damp cowboy gown neatly under the sheet and pull my blanket around my shoulders. "What have you got for me that's so important you woke me up in the middle of the night?" I say.

His red hair is greasy, and his black shirt has mustard—or something yellow—dripped down the front. He shakes his head. "Richard," he says. "I cannot condone—"

I lean forward and push the call button on my bed. Then I point a finger in his fat face. "Who asked you? Who asked you to condone anything? I want you out of my room, now." I'm yelling and losing my breath, but I keep on yelling. "Whatever happened to privacy, man? That's a basic human right, and you violate it every time you come in here, don't even knock, and start preaching your crap. I have rights, man. I do not have to be subjected to this—"

"Richard, what is it?" Jeannette is in the doorway.

"It's him," I yell. "He comes in here, without even knocking, and he forces me to listen to his bullshit. Make him get out. I want to be left alone."

Br'er Bertrand stands up. He's shaking, and if anyone ever wanted to smack a sick kid, it's him. His face is purple. "You were hardly alone, were you?" Spit flies in my direction. He flings himself around, spitting toward Jeannette. "She was naked!" he says. "In this boy's bed!"

Jeannette comes in and puts a hand on the Br'er's chest. "Just leave," she says. "You're upsetting my patient."

The man sort of deflates, then he points at a big envelope that he dropped on the floor. "I was simply delivering this," he says. "A package from the boy's uncle. That is all. And this is the thanks I get." And he turns and walks out, his butt held so tight that even his pants are clenched.

Jeannette puts her hands over her face and rubs, hard. "She was naked?" she says. "Let me get this straight. You had a naked girl in your bed with you? Now I wonder. Who might that little Lady Godiva be?" She comes over and lifts my hand, feeling my pulse. "God, boy, you're going to have a heart attack. Lean back, now. You got to relax, Richard. Calm down, now. Breathe."

I lean back and take some breaths. I'm dizzy as all hell, it's true.

She waits until my heartbeat slows down and then she sighs. "Okay, now you want to tell me what's going on here? And, please Lord, say it's not something that's going to get me fired. You came real close last time, with your little tricks." She sits down on the chair. "I'm tired, son. I really am. So just spit it out."

I nod. "I don't know why that guy makes me so mad, but he does. Like, he just barges in, middle of the night and—"

"Richard, it's seven thirty P.M., that's all. I know that because it means I'm only four and a half hours into my shift, with three and a half to go."

"Huh," I say. "Thought it was much later." How, I think, could all of that happen in a few hours? Kelly-Marie and Sylvie and everything? Like my whole life changed in, what, a flash? Like time is getting compressed or something? Like I've gone into warp speed? Entirely possible. Even makes a kind of strange sense, time altering its flow in this place.

"Yeah, well, that's not important. I repeat, *who* was naked in here? What *she* was in here, anyway?"

I close my eyes and say, with dignity, "I cannot reveal that. My mama raised a gentleman."

She actually starts to laugh and she stands up. "Right. But let me say one thing, Mr. Prince-Among-Men. If you

124

happen to be fooling around with that Sylvie girl, her daddy is going to skin you like a rabbit. And put you in a stew. Although," she kind of mutters to herself, "how much harm you two can do, in your state, well . . ." She clicks her tongue. "Just don't do it on my shift, okay? Please, please, please."

I open my eyes, and her brown face is soft. "Sylvie says she's going to get better," I say, real quiet. "She totally believes it. You think that's possible?"

Her lips go still and she shakes her head. "Oh, honey. I don't know."

"What are the odds?"

She sighs. "Odds? I don't go by odds. Not anymore. I've seen too much." She bends over my bed, straightening the sheets.

"Jeannette, do you ever, you know, pray?"

"Huh. Pray? That's a good question. I guess I might, but I don't assume I got God's ear, you know, like some people do. I mean, look where I work. How the heck would I know who to pray for around here?"

I nod. Now that's a problem, isn't it? Who would you pray for tonight, for example? The guy who walked out of Bataan umpteen years ago and just tonight his number's up? Or his roommate? The woman in the coma? Or Mrs. Elkins? Sylvie? Me?

She puts a hand flat on my chest. "Now I think of it, you know who I might pray for, if I were so inclined?" she asks.

I look at her. "Who?"

"Sylvia's father, that's who. I have never seen a man in so much pain."

Sylvie's father. Now that is a surprise. That's someone I never thought worthy of prayer. I shake my head. "Don't waste your time," I say. "That man's a demon."

"No. That man's in hell, is all. He's not in charge of the place, he's just been thrown in there. Given no choice and having no options. Think about that. Man's used to taking care of his family, his child. Protecting them, you know? And now . . . Well, now." She turns away, all brisk and nurselike. "Now, young man, I think you need a clean gown, and I'm not speculating on why, that's for sure. And maybe you'd like some Jell-O. Edward's report says you say you want to eat a little. Red or green?"

NEXT MORNING, I'M UP and showered and dressed and I've had my little breakfast of broth and coffee, nice and early, just like I actually have something to do, a real busy day ahead of me. There's sunshine outside the windows, and I'm feeling decent. I pick up the package that Br'er Bertrand left. The aide that cleaned up my room left it on the night table.

It's a big envelope, the padded kind. Inside, on top, there's a note. It's obvious, right away, that it's from Uncle Phil—the handwriting is all bold and messy, and the paper smells like him, cigarette smoke and beer. *Your Majesty*, it starts. *Sorry I had to abandon you. Had to get out of Dodge, pronto. But sat up all night long, working on these. I'll be back real soon, I promise.* He signed it, *Your loyal lackey, Philip the Fool.* Then there's a PS: *I trust you'll find the secret clues, my lord.*

I pull out the sheets of thick paper, each one ragged on top, like they were ripped out of one of those big artist's pads you can buy. They're drawings, charcoal I think at first. But then I realize that they must be pen and ink, the lines are so fine. Black-and-white, no color. The top one is labeled *The Woman in the Coma. October 31.* Funny, his writing here is perfectly neat and square. Like once he goes into artist mode, Phil's a different guy. I'm almost scared to look real close at the picture, so I take a few minutes to spread all of them out on top of my bed. There's five altogether. They've all got labels and dates: *Family Lounge. October 31. The Two Old Guys, Room 304. October 31. Sylvia. October 31. Richie's World. October 31.*

My heart, for some reason, is up high in my throat, just glancing at the pictures. They're really detailed, so finely drawn that there are, like, hundreds of details in each one. I don't know why drawings should scare me, but they do. It's like, I don't know, like I'll see things I don't want to know. Like, in black-and-white, the reality of this place will be too much. But there they are, on my bed, all in a row, and I think how wussy it would be not to study them, appreciate all Phil's work, anyway. I mean, it's clear the guy's got a gift. And that he worked like hell on these. But they're hard to take, all at once. So I pile them up, in an order that seems to me to be least to most scary, least on top. You know, so I can look at a couple and leave the rest, if I want to.

I lean over *The Woman in a Coma* and try to figure it out. All the angles are weird, like everything in the room radiates out from one central spot. Everything's there: the windows, the door, the ceiling, the walls, the bed table with its suction equipment, all of that. But it's like, all circular. And it's all kind of distorted, like everything is pulling toward you. Everything is sort of being sucked in. Those little border cherubs, they're all stretched out and weird, like gargoyles or something. I keep staring. And then I get it: everything in the picture is from *her* point of view. Like she's the one standing outside the picture, looking in. There's a kind of tingling in my head as I fall into what Phil's done: he's put me in her place. *I'm* the woman in the coma, and this is what I see. It's freaky as all hell, but I can't stop looking. The more I look, the more I notice. There are little faces scattered around the room, tiny, like flies. All the mouths are open, they're chattering at me, but I can't tell what they're saying. After a while, I see what's outside the window. It's the moon, a fat full moon. Inside it, there's a bigger face. And it's grinning, big jack-o'-lantern grin, two pointy teeth on top, one on the bottom. I'm not sure whether it's a happy grin or an evil grin. I stare into the Moon Man's eyes for a minute and I still can't decide. I have to roll back from the bed, I'm so dizzy. If there's a secret clue here, I don't get it.

I roll back up and pull out the old guys one. It's sort of happy: there are two guys sitting up in bed, watching the TV on the wall. Each guy's got a beer in one hand and a cigarette in the other. I look again. These guys are young; their faces are, anyway. They've got hair and scruffy whiskers and no wrinkles. One's wearing a Yankees cap, and the other one some kind of beat-up fishing hat, full of tied flies. The one in the cap is pointing at the TV with his smoke, laughing. I follow the line of his pointing hand and I can see what's on: there are guys in white shorts and guys in black shorts, all watching as a soccer ball goes into the net. When I look back at the old guys, I see what I missed the first time: they're not in beds; they're in recliner chairs. Scattered around the chairs are copies of *Playboy* and *Sports Illustrated*. And the walls, they're not hospital walls, either. There's wallpaper and framed pictures on the walls and bookshelves full of sports trophies and school pictures of kids and all of that. I shake my head and smile. Those guys are home, in a family rec room or something. Just regular guys, watching TV and hanging out.

This isn't so bad. I'm pulling out the family lounge one when Sylvie's voice fills the room. "Hey. Good morning, Rich-Man," she says.

I turn around and wave her in from the doorway. She looks tired, but she's still walking on her own. She's wearing a short plaid skirt over black leggings, with a white blouse and little flat black shoes. Total prep-school girl.

"Hey. You look like you're off to school."

She runs a hand down the skirt. "Yep. Any day now." She comes in. "What are those?"

I'm kind of proud of the pictures, because they show that someone in my family has some sort of talent. "Drawings my uncle Phil did. They're pretty amazing. I only showed him around once, and he, like, got it. Come look."

She comes and stands next to me, leaning over the back of my chair. She stares down at the picture of the guys in 304. "Wow," she says. "Very cool." All of a sudden she points to a framed picture on the wall of the room the two guys are sitting in. "Look what this says."

I put my face almost right on the paper, but I can't read the tiny words she's pointing at. I mean, I can see that maybe there are words there, but it's like some half-invisible ink or something, blurry.

She gets impatient. "Come on, Richard, are you blind? Look, it's like some little embroidered motto thing." She taps her finger on the paper. "Look. It says *Forever Young* in script. And there's a flower border around it."

I sit up and shrug. "If you say so." It bothers me a

little, that Sylvie's eyes are still okay. That she's that much stronger than me. I mean, I know that she still texts her friends all the time. Won't let them come visit, but texts giggly, happy little messages to all of them. It is, actually, a pretty cool way of lying. What they can't see can't hurt them, right? Little screens are all they see. And whatever she wants them to know.

"It's right there," she says. "And it's sort of sweet, don't you think?"

"Yeah," I say. But, really, I don't know about that. The only way to stay forever young, if you think about it, is to die before you get old, right? But I don't say that. Instead, I ask her to look at the woman in the coma one. Maybe she'll find the clue there, too.

It doesn't take her a second. "Whoa," she says. "That's, like, psychedelic, man." She points at the smiling man in the moon. "There's one word on each of his teeth, see? Tiny little capital letters: LONG TIME GONE." She shakes her head. "Ain't that the truth. That woman is *so* not here. Long time gone is right. Let's see another one."

We both stare into the family lounge. It's just like it is in real life, dusty flowers and all. But there's a middle-aged couple sitting on the couch, staring at the TV screen. She's all prissy-dressed in a flowered blouse and plain skirt, feet crossed at the ankles; he's in a suit and tie, shiny black dress shoes on his feet. The only thing that's weird that I can see is that there's a little bunch of cherub angel things—you know, fat babies with white feathery wings—hovering over their shoulders. And in the corner, the harpy, bent over her harp, strumming her heart out. And she's got white feathery wings, too. It seems sort of sweet to me.

But Sylvie is holding her sides, laughing. She points at the TV. I can't see what she's laughing at until she says, "Look what they're watching. Porn!"

I still can't see it—it's just a bunch of tiny lines all sort of twisted together—but I laugh anyway. "No kidding!"

She points to a VCR tape holder on the floor at the couple's feet. Even she has to put her nose on the paper to read the letters on it. "And look at the name of the tape: *The Screw-Yourself-to-a-Cure Hospital Handbook*. And look..." Her finger touches the man's suit-pants. "He's got a hard-on—see it? It's clear as day under his pants, a real boner. And her hand here is, like, creeping under her skirt. She's touching herself!" She shakes her head. "Your uncle is a riot."

"Sure is," I say. I wish I could see it, but, what the hell, hearing Sylvie talk dirty is almost better. "You want to see the next one?" I forget what that one is and pull it out.

Sylvie gets real quiet when she sees it's her: *Sylvia, October 31.*

133

I get to see most of it before she picks it up and holds it against her chest. It's all of those pictures of Sylvia as a baby and as a girl and as an athlete and award-winner and all of that, made into a frame around a bed. The girl in the bed is asleep, curled up on her side, naked. She's gorgeous: long curly black hair, full breasts, sweet round ass. I look again: I think I see a baby held against one breast. But then Sylvie's got the picture completely hidden. I look at her face and there are tears running down her cheeks. "Hey," I say. I touch her shoulder. "Does it have a clue?"

She looks at me like I'm the dumbest person she's ever met. "It *is* the clue, Richard, the whole thing." She holds it out again for a minute. "Don't you see? It's me, grown up. With a baby. It's, like, my future. See, Richard? I grow up. I make it." She points to the bottom of the paper. "It says *Pretty Woman.*"

She holds the picture against her as she walks out of the room. She's keeping it cradled up against her chest, like that picture is the baby she's going to have someday.

I have a few minutes of being mad at Uncle Phil. I mean, what right does the guy have to imagine her naked? Or, even worse, to give her false hope? I mean, I hate that, I really do. Sure, I spout the magic-science-geek-miracle-cure crap when I have to—but I don't *believe* it. And I don't want to hope, either. I mean, I want to know. I want to know and face it and deal with it. Okay?

So why is my heart pounding when I pull out the last picture, *Richie's World*? I mean, what do I expect? A crystal ball? A glimpse of my future? Shit, I know Phil. He's no soothsayer, believe me. If he were, he wouldn't mess up his own life right and left, right? I mean, he'd see all those disasters coming and he'd duck. That's what I think. But what I feel? I don't know, that's different. I bend over the picture and see that it's much simpler than the rest. It's me, in my wheelchair, from the back. I'm big, in the center of the page. Everything else around me is tiny, like I'm high above it. But it's still easy to see the hallway and the rooms and the nurses' station and all. It's this place, but it's way below. And beyond that, even, is what looks like a map: the Hudson River curving away, going far off into the distance that I can't really see. I look at me again: I'm wearing my Halloween getup, the crown on my head and the blanket-cape around my shoulders. But the cape is much longer, all sort of flowing out behind me, the stars on the fabric kind of melting into the stars that are scattered all over the page. I've got both my arms out straight in front of me like Superman used to in all those TV shows. The letters on my cape are big enough even for me to read: *Richard Casey: The Incredible Flying Boy.*

I look at it for a long time. It's funny, the longer I look, the more I feel like I actually am flying, like I'm lifting off. It's sort of fun and big-time scary, that feeling. Sort of comforting and totally terrifying, watching everything here get smaller and smaller and smaller. Houston, we have liftoff. Over and out.

When I'm so dizzy I have to look away, I spend some time just staring out the window into the bright blue sky. Shit, I think, holy shit. I pick up *Richie's World* and put it back into the envelope. I find a pen and write on the front: *For Sisco (aka Richie's mom), with love from her brother, Phil.* Then I roll to the little closet by the door and I stash the envelope under my gym bag and the other stuff I brought with me. Mom will find it, I figure, later. Maybe she'll hate it—but maybe not.

The other pictures, the dirty ones and the funny ones? Those I hang on my bulletin board for everyone to see. Then I roll to Sylvie's room and look in. She's sitting on the edge of her bed, still dressed for school. Only now she's added a hat, a black beret tilted on her head, and a black jacket. No one's with her; her mother and bros must be taking another day off. She looks like she's waiting for something, or someone, to pick her up and take her on a date, take her somewhere, anyway. I just can't stand it if she keeps on sitting there, all dressed up with nowhere to go. That's just not right. So I roll into the room and say, "Hey, Pretty Woman. Want to blow this joint?"

And before you can say "Jack Robinson," she's on her feet and pushing my chair toward the lobby and the elevator. I try to help her by pushing the wheels myself, but she slaps my hands away. I know that Edward sees us; he's right there at the nurses' station, writing in the charts, and we're sort of hard to miss. But he doesn't make eye contact and he doesn't say a thing.

In the lobby, the harpy looks up but never once stops strumming. She smiles. "Hello, children," she says. "Have a blessed day."

Sylvie's reply echoes all the way down in the elevator. I won't repeat it here, though, because it's really shocking and totally gross.

THERE ARE A WHOLE lot of funny looks as we pass through the corridors on the first floor by the lobby, I got to admit. This is where ordinary citizens of the world come in and out, for blood tests or X-rays or whatever. Sylvie's fuzzy head is covered with her little black beret, but mine is just hanging out there in the open for everyone to gawk at. Most people, though, they're sort of naturally polite. They take one good gawk and then their eyes shift down to the floor, like they're really following the blue or the orange or the red lines that lead them to where they're going. Little kids are more up-front. They point. But that's okay, because Sylvie points back, with her hand shaped like a gun, and goes, "POW" to each and every kid. She uses her thumb like a trigger, and the kids either giggle or frown.

Of course, she also wants to stop in the gift shop. It's ridiculous. I mean, what could we possibly need? This is what I say to her: "Oh, come on. You want to buy get-well cards?"

Sylvie shakes her head. "You are such a *boy*, Richard. I'm here to shop, not buy. This is the closest thing I've got to the mall. I'm *shopping*." So she rolls me in there and parks me in a far corner, and I sit for what seems like three or four days while she browses around, picking up and putting down every object in the place, sweartogod. She's humming and she touches every last thing. Every package of gum, every magazine, every potted plant, every stuffed animal, each and every card. The old lady with a pink volunteer smock behind the counter smiles at Sylvie—for a while. Then she starts to tap her fingers on the cash register. "May I help you, dear?" she says. "Are you looking for anything special?"

Sylvie flashes me a sharp-toothed smile. But to the woman at the counter, she gives a shy little nod. "Oh thank you, ma'am. Yes, I am. I'd like something for my sister. She just had a baby."

The woman narrows her eyes. "Your sister?"

"Oh, yes. My older sister." She leans over the counter and smiles like an angel. "She married our minister's son last year, and now the Lord has blessed them with a daughter. Do you have any really cute stuffed seals? My sister's crazy about seals."

The woman smiles and pats Sylvie's hand. "How sweet you are. Let me check. I do remember that we had a baby seal once. It was white, with blue eyes. Maybe in the back." And she scoots behind a curtain.

In the fifteen or so seconds that the volunteer lady's gone, Sylvie lifts, like, eight packs of gum and whooshes me out of there. We sit in the ER waiting room for a while, chewing. Well, she's chewing. I just sort of suck on my gum; I wouldn't ever tell her, but my teeth are all kind of loose, and gum isn't exactly my thing these days. When she's not looking, I take the gum out of my mouth and toss it in an ashtray. Then she spits her big glob into a plastic plant and says, "Okay, enough stalling. We need to get outside, into the air. Ready?"

I am so ready.

The sun is bright and the sky is blue. But the wind, which of course we couldn't see from the inside, is a bitch. It's cold and sharp and full of city grit. Sylvie can't push me into it for more than five feet at a time, it's so strong. We make it as far as the little glass smoking shelter outside the ER. And I have to wheel myself the last ten yards, because Sylvie is breathing so hard and her legs are shaking.

Once we get inside there, though, it's not so bad. Nobody else is in here—who would be crazy enough to brave hurricane winds just for a smoke? But inside, we're out of the wind and it's bearable. Sylvie's shivering all over. She climbs into my lap, and I wrap the blanket around her. She tucks her head onto my shoulder, and we both look out through the smudgy glass walls. At least we can see something different from here. Sure, it's mostly the ER parking lot and three houses across the street and, if we lean, a tiny bit of the river, way off down the hill. It stinks of smoke and wet butts piled in the metal ashtray thing. That's okay, too—I mean, those are smells you just don't get around hospice. Even the stink lets us know we're somewhere else, that we got out. "I want you to appreciate that I take you to only the best places," I say, putting my lips right against her neck.

She laughs. "Yes, indeed." She wriggles around on my lap, getting more comfortable. Her sharp hip bones kind of hurt, but it's a nice kind of hurt, and I tighten my arms around her. She points at one of the houses across the street. It's just a typical Hudson house, three stories, town house sort of thing, kind of old and made of brick painted white, with black shutters. The paint is peeling, and the whole thing looks kind of saggy. But it's got a big front porch and the people haven't moved the summer chairs inside yet. There's still a little bit of green on the square front lawn and a few brown leaves on the oak tree to the side. "Let's live there, Richard," she says, "when we get married.

Okay? I mean, just as a starter house. Before we move to a much nicer place, outside of town."

My throat gets tight, just picturing it. "Sure," I say. "You got it."

She nods. "The living room has a fireplace. There's the chimney. See? So on a cold day like today, you'll make a fire, right? Well, not until the evening, when we're both home from our jobs and can sit on the couch and put our feet up and drink our wine and talk about our days. And you'll keep it going all evening, until it's really late and we're sleepy and warm and ready to go to bed. Okay?"

"Yes, ma'am," I say. "I'll keep that fire going as long as you want. But when it's time to go to bed . . . ? Tell me about that."

She slaps a hand on my chest. "Oh, sure. That's all you men think about. Going to bed." She squiggles her hips a little more and then laughs when she feels Bingo rising up against her bottom. Her voice drops into a sexy whisper. "Well, Richard. Let me start by saying that our bed is very large. King-size. Four-poster, with one of those big lace canopies on top, going from post to post. And it's got tons of pillows—all the best down—and six-hundred-count cotton sheets and a fluffy down duvet and—"

"Six hundred what? And what the hell is a duvet?"

She slaps me again. "Ignorant male. It's a comforter.

And the sheets are very smooth. Shut up. Let me talk."
She presses against me. "So, we take off our clothes and
that makes us shiver a little, because it's chilly upstairs,
right? And then we rush to get under the covers, and we
both—quick, quick, quick—we slide right to the center of
that big old bed, where we meet. Actually, there's this little
dip in the mattress, right in the center, because that's where
we always meet, you know? When we're naked and in our
bed. And, well, let's just say that the bedsprings there are a
little worn down, from all the bouncing, and—"

"We bounce?" I push myself up against her and close
my eyes.

"Oh, yeah, we do. Sometimes, mister, *you* bounce so
hard that I think I'm going to fly up into that lace canopy,
and I have to hang on really tight and I have to, like, clench
my legs around you and—"

"You're on top?"

She almost purrs. "Of course I'm on top, Richard. I'm
in charge." She turns herself around on my lap so that she's
straddling me. She pulls up her skirt and puts a knee on
each side of my hips. Then she reaches in and shoves down
my sweatpants. Now when she settles herself, I find the
warm, damp spot I'm dying for, just the other side of her
panties. I wrap my arms and the blanket around us, holding on tight, so she's invisible under there, her head tucked

143

into my chest. "So," she says, and now her voice is kind of rough. "So there we are. I tease you, a little bit, by moving away." She pulls her hips away for a second, then she brings them down against me again, firm. She's warmer, and the panties are slipping, slipping to one side. "And then I come back," she says.

I am that close. That close to being inside her. There are circles of light pressed against my eyelids and every muscle in my body is straining toward her.

The air in the glass enclosure changes and I can tell someone's come in, even before I hear the voice say, "Richie. My god, Richie. What are you doing out here?"

Sylvie goes still and then she pulls away. Her hands reach down and arrange her panties. She grabs my sweatpants and hauls them up. Then she takes her hands away and she puts her head up through the opening in the blanket. "Hey," she says. "Can't you see we'd like a little privacy here? Who are you?"

But I already know who it is: I recognized the voice and I opened my eyes the minute I heard it. I look at the tall woman with the bright red hair and a cigarette dangling from bright red lips. I say, "Hi, Grandma."

And Sylvie goes, "Jesus H. Christ," and climbs out of my lap.

There's a long sort of silence, and then Grandma bends

down and picks up Sylvie's beret from the dirty cement floor of the shelter. "You dropped this, sweetie," she says. "Sorry to interrupt."

Sylvie pulls the beret over her fuzzy head. She waves a hand, like Queen Elizabeth dismissing a clumsy footman. "No problem," she says. "Can I have a smoke?"

I'm kind of choking over that "no problem" since I am, wilted or not, still on fire. But no one's paying any attention to me, none whatsoever. These girls are bonding and I'm no one, I can tell.

Grandma pulls out a pack of Marlboros and hands one to Sylvie, even lights it for her, with a bright green plastic Bic lighter.

Sylvie sucks in smoke, long and hard. I watch her eyes close and her throat work. This is clearly not a novice smoker; this is a hardcore addict if I ever saw one. When she opens her eyes, she smiles. "God, that's better than sex, anyway." She pats my head, like I'm three years old. "Oh, don't look so miserable, Richard. That's what adolescent sex is all about, right? Ninety-five percent frustration. Totally normal teenage encounter, incomplete and unsatisfying. You'll live."

Grandma gives a snort and bends to kiss the top of my head. "It's so good to see you, sweetheart," she says. "And your girlfriend is right. No one ever died from frustration."

145

She takes a long drag from her cigarette and smiles at Sylvie.

They are ganging up on me, totally. Girls against boy. Smokers vs. nonsmoker. I roll my eyes. "Maybe not. But some people might die *before* they ever get laid." I put my hands on my wheels. "It's cold. I'm going in. Excuse me, please." I roll between them and out into the wind. I can hear them clucking as I fight my way back inside the building, slowly. By the time I make it through the sliding glass doors, Grandma is right behind me.

She grabs the handles and starts pushing. She turns back to Sylvie. "Hop on, honey," she says. "You look beat."

Sylvie does hop on, but it's nothing like before. Now she perches on my bony knees, facing forward, like she's some sort of figurehead woman on the prow of a ship. Like she's that wooden and that hard. She glares at people as we go by. Totally against hospital rules, she's still got her cigarette in her mouth and she's blowing smoke all the way. And no one dares to say a word.

Until we get to the hospice floor. Grandma has given one good shriek at the sight of the harpy and hustled us right onto the floor. Mrs. Lee, the floor clerk, the one who ate the Good & Plenty on Halloween, she leaps from behind her desk and grabs the cigarette out of Sylvie's mouth. "What are you *thinking*?" she gasps, wrapping the still-burning butt in her hand and throwing it on the floor, where she stamps it into oblivion. "Good lord, girl, there are people on oxygen here. Do you want to blow us all sky-high?"

That's a question I'm afraid that Sylvie might actually answer. She's holding on to my kneecaps with both hands and I can feel her trembling. I smile nicely at Mrs. Lee. "Sorry," I say. "Foolish of us. Kids today! What are you going to do?"

She does not smile back. She glares at Grandma. "You, presumably, are an adult, ma'am. Although one wouldn't think so. Do you have permission to visit this floor? May I see your visitor's pass?"

I start to say, "Hey, that's my grandmother," but Grandma's got it covered.

"Richard Casey is my grandson," she says, tapping her bright red fingernails on Mrs. Lee's desk. "And this lovely child is his friend, who we are returning to her room, safe and sound. No harm done. Surely you can just give me a pass. Grandmothers are always allowed. Right, sweetheart?" She winks at me.

Mrs. Lee's eyes shoot daggers, but she hands a bright orange visitor's pass to Grandma and off we go. We bring Sylvie to her room, and Grandma has to help her into her bed. Sylvie looks floppy now, like a rag doll dressed in a school uniform. Grandma pulls the curtains and I hear her sort of murmuring to Sylvie and I hear the sounds of clothes being slipped off and sheets being pulled up. I just sit there, feeling pretty damn unneeded. "Hey, ladies," I say after a while. "I'm going to split. See you around." And I roll back to my room, where I'm not sure I can get myself into bed, either. But I've learned some tricks of the trade and I manage to haul myself from the chair by hanging on to the side of the bed and using the railings like a step-ladder to climb in. I'm so sleepy that there's not three seconds between hitting the sheets and unconsciousness.

* * *

When I come to, Grandma is sitting in the chair by my bed, her hands over her eyes. I take a minute to look over her while she's not looking at me. I figure out how old she is: Mom was seventeen when I was born and Grandma was sixteen when Mom was born. And I'm seventeen now. Do a little addition in the head: Grandma must be fifty! But she's still got tons of orangey-red hair and she's still skinny and she's still wearing high heels and tight black pants. Her shirt is bright green and shiny and unbuttoned three buttons down, and there's plenty of freckled, wrinkly cleavage there. She's got about a hundred chains and beads and whatnot around her neck and about a hundred more around each wrist. Fifteen rings on bony fingers. Grandma's been a hostess at a club in Scotch Plains, New Jersey, forever, and she dresses pretty much the same, on the job or off. I've got to smile: the difference between my mom and her mom is just amazing. My mom, she's got blonde hair that she wears straight and plain, to her shoulders. Never seen her in makeup or heels. She wears longish cotton skirts to work, with crisp button-down shirts and cardigan sweaters. I heard one of her friends once tell her how pretty she'd be if she made an effort, and I heard Mom tell her to buzz off. Grandma's always after her to brighten up, too. "You look like you took a vow of chastity, honey," I once heard Grandma say. "Like you're packed and ready for the nunnery." And Mom only smiled. "I did," she said. "Day Richie was born, I took that vow. I'm too busy for all that nonsense. So leave me alone."

Grandma drops her hands and I see that her eye makeup is runny and that she's been crying. When she sees me awake, she quickly grabs a handful of Kleenex from her pocket and blows her nose. She dabs under her eyes, and the Kleenex come back all black. She stands up and kisses me on the head. "Hey, there, Richie Rich." She leans over and hugs my head to her chest. I smell perfume and hair spray, cigarettes and a little bit of sweat.

Richie Rich. This is a name she always called me.

149

Some kid from an old comic, I understand. Real rich kid. She always said I'd have millions myself, someday, smart as I was. Seemed cute, once upon a time. Seems like a stupid joke now. I weasel my head out of her grip. "Hey. How's Mom?"

She sits back down and shakes her head. "Feverish. Coughing. Cranky. Crazy to get in here. Worried nearly to death about you. Total pain in the ass. Otherwise, she's okay."

"Oh." I realize that I don't want to hear, really, about how my mom is. It's too sad. "So," I say, "when'd you arrive?"

"Last night, late. I've been packed for weeks, waiting for her to call. Grabbed the bus from Plainfield to the city, then the train up here. Got here, took a cab straight to the house. She was a tiny bit glad to see me, I think." She smiles, showing yellow crooked teeth. "Mostly so I could check up on you, young man. She thinks you might get up to something while she's not here. Get in trouble. What a silly thought, huh?" She pokes a sharp red nail into my leg.

I shrug. "Phil get home?" I ask.

"No. I haven't a clue where your uncle is at the moment. Par for the course." She sits up straight and looks around the room. "So, what do you do for fun around here? Besides trying to get in that pretty little girl's pants, I mean?"

"Not a lot," I say. "Pretty quiet around here."

"Huh. I'd go out of my gourd. Well, let's see what's on TV, okay?" She clicks on the set and then settles down with Oprah. Perfect cue for Richie Rich to drop back to sleep—and so I do.

***

When I wake up again, the sky outside my window is dark. The wind is still out there, though—I can hear it howling, even through the glass, and every once in a while something smooches against the window, some leaves or plastic bag or something. Wild night. I sit up. The TV is now burbling on about bridezillas and Grandma is sound asleep, all scrunched up in the chair. I got to pee and I try to get out of bed without waking her, but she sits straight up the second my feet hit the floor.

She groans, holding her back and trying to stretch out. "Jesus," she says. "I am too old to sleep like that. Hey, kiddo, you need any help?"

I hate to think that I've gotten to the point of asking my grandmother to help me pee. "No, thanks," I say. I pause on my way to the bathroom, hanging on to the back of her chair for balance. "Why don't you go on home, Grandma? See how Mom's doing? I'm worried about her."

She shakes her head. "Nope. I got my orders. She told

151

me to park my ass right here, watch over you like a hawk. Not to leave you alone for five seconds. She said she'd skin me alive if you got into any more trouble on my watch."

She stands up and puts both hands at her back, moaning. "Sorry—I know you'd like privacy, Richard. I really do understand, and I sympathize. But I'm just following orders here, son. Following orders."

I give her a sarcastic salute. "Yes, sir, ma'am. Ma'am. Permission to pee, ma'am?"

She laughs, then goes into a hawking, smoky cough. "Granted," she wheezes out. "Go for it."

When I get back and sit on the edge of the bed, she's got cards spread out on the bed table, solitaire formation. She's turning and slapping cards down so fast that it makes me dizzy to watch. Her hands fly, and she gives little grunts whenever a card she's been looking for comes up.

I sit for a while, quiet, and then I say what I've been thinking about. It's funny, because I don't even know that I've been thinking about this, really, until the words come out of my mouth. "Hey, Grandma," I go. "Do you think my father might want to know about me?" Her eyes come up so fast and so wide that I have to rush on with what, suddenly, I know that I want to say. "I mean, maybe? I don't know who the guy is, even; you know Mom, she won't say a word about it, but I figure you might. I was going to ask

Phil, but we got all involved in other stuff and I don't know if he even knows. But I always got the feeling that you *do* know, and I thought that..." I run out of breath.

Grandma goes back to turning cards over, but much slower now, and I can almost hear her thinking. She keeps her eyes on the cards. She's piled up a whole lot of red cards on black cards when she finally says, "It's weird that you say that. I've been thinking hard about that same thing, Richard. Your mother would kill me, I know it. But I—well, I've been considering."

My heart goes real still in my chest. "So, you do know?"

She puts down another card: black four on red five. "I do. I always have. Or at least I'm pretty damn sure." She looks up at me, and her black-smudged eyes are, I don't know exactly, full of pissed-off sadness. "Your mom doesn't know I know. Oh, she suspects, and once or twice I told her she was crazy for not getting the child support she's entitled to, for not nailing the guy's skin to a tree and getting some help, for Christ sake. But not her. No. She struggled to take care of you and herself, and I swear sometimes you two damn near starved. But never once did she disturb that man's cozy little oh-so-happy life."

I fold my hands on my lap so they'll stop shaking. "So, he has a happy life?"

She shrugs and starts up with the cards again. Red

three on black four. "How the hell do I know? Who the hell really knows anything about anybody's life?" She slaps the ace of hearts up above the rows of cards. "All right. I'll admit that I looked the guy up online a couple times and the pictures looked happy. But whose don't?"

"So, does he still live around here?"

She adds the two of hearts to the ace and then takes the red three she just put on the black four and moves it up there, too. Her game is going really well. "Nope. Not anymore. He moved away the summer before you were born. Convenient, huh?"

This sort of feels like an arrow in my chest. "Did he know? That I was coming? That why he left?"

She shakes her head. "Aha—got you, ace of clubs!" She puts that one up above the other cards. Damned if she isn't going to win this game. "I very much doubt it. Close-mouthed girl like your mom, what do you think?"

I think that never in a million years would my mom have told the guy if she thought he didn't want her and the baby, if he didn't have room in his life for us. Never in a billion years. "Yeah. He didn't know. Right. Not his fault, I guess."

She slams a palm down on the table. "Not his fault? Baloney. She was sixteen, Richard, when she got knocked up. Sixteen years old, quiet, shy, gentle as a lamb. And he was one of her teachers at Hudson High School. A married man. English teacher. Read poems to her, put stars in her eyes. I remember how she looked all that winter. Like she was floating in the clouds. New books in her backpack every day. All she talked about, day and night, was poetry and 'she walks in beauty like the night' and all of that crap. Oh, yeah, that man was some teacher. He certainly did *educate* that child, didn't he? And, oopsie, put a bun in her belly, free of charge. And that's not his fault? Charm the kid by spouting verse and then stick it to her? God al-fucking-mighty." She stands up and the cards fly all over the bed, some slipping to the floor. She's shaking. "And now he's a big shot down in Westchester. School superintendent, some shit like that. Bastard." She turns and walks out of the room.

I lean back on the pillows and think. I mean, I don't *feel* anything, not really, but my head's all super-clear and I can think. Think hard. My mom is going to be real lonely, I figure, sometime soon. And she's going to need all kinds of help. Money, that's always a help. I mean, it's not everything, not even half of what she deserves. But it's a help. When Grandma comes back in, carrying my supper tray, I sit up and say, "Listen, Grandma. You can do it. You can

155

get yourself a lawyer and you can just ask: hey, could we find this guy and make him pay up? Little DNA test, whatever. And if it's him, whammo. I mean, like, eighteen years of back child support, from a guy with a good job, that's a whole lot, right? That would set Mom up for life. Could you do that?"

She puts the tray down. "Oh, Richard, I don't know. She would be so angry."

I reach over and grab Grandma's hand. "For a while, maybe, she'd be pissed, yeah. But I'm giving you my permission, all right? I mean, I have some say in all of this. And I want to think she'll be okay. Okay? I mean, that's real, real important to me. I got to think she'll be okay." I can feel that my voice is getting shaky and I can see that she's about to bawl, too. "Just do it, okay?"

She pulls the silver cover off the food. "God, is this what they call food?" She picks up a fork and takes a taste of the meat. "Lord." She takes another bite. Then she sets the fork down, real gentle. She squeezes my hand. "I'll think about it, Richie. But no promises. I'll ponder, on my own. It's not like she likes me all that much right now, right? Like she isn't mad at me all the time anyhow. But don't bug me anymore. Do not say one more word about it. Anyhoo . . ." she tosses her hair back and laughs. I can tell it's costing her something, that laugh, but she's a tough lady. You got to give that to the women in my family: they are both hugely tough in their different ways. Not so different, maybe, after all.

"Deal," I say. "Thanks."

She waves a hand in the air, dismissing the whole subject. She hands me a cup of coffee and digs into the potatoes. "What? Don't make that face," she says. "Sure, the food stinks, but it's free. I don't turn down free food, no way." There's a few minutes of quiet while I sip and she chews. Then she looks at me and her eyes are shiny and sort of sparkly, and I can see that something wicked and entertaining is about to happen. "And, Richard, here's something else I've been thinking about, much more fun. I had a brainstorm. Well, the idea came from that smart little Miss Sylvie, really. Something she came up with while I was getting her back into bed. She's a pisser, that one. You want to hear it?"

I smile. "Sure. What's Sylvie's idea?"

Grandma grins like a kid. "Well, Sylvie thought that maybe I could, let us say, distract her father for a while this evening. She says that he needs a drink, goes out almost every evening for a bit once she's asleep. She thinks that I might ask to accompany the man, might keep him out a wee bit longer than usual. So that you two can have, let us say, some free time together? And some privacy?" She winks. "What do you think?"

I close my eyes. "What I think is that I have the best grandma on earth," I say.

"Don't I know it. Let's just call it an early birthday gift, kiddo."

I DECIDE TO TAKE a shower. I mean, personal hygiene is right up there in terms of studliness for women, right? Don't want to offend. Women like their partners—this is the word the health teachers use, *partners*—to smell good, I've heard. They are, in fact, ridiculously picky about this sort of thing. Thus, a shower is in order. This is easier decided than done, however. Edward isn't on duty, and there really isn't anyone else I can ask for help. Nobody showers at night, and any nurse I ask to help is going to wonder why I'm so hot for cleanliness at this precise moment. It's a dilemma. I am not going to resort to Grandma, and anyway, she's off down the hall, chatting up Sylvie's father, I assume, making friends. Probably flirting like hell, it occurs to me. She's not so much older than him and she's still kind of a looker—I mean, for a grandma. That is so weird and disturbing a thought that I go back to working on how to accomplish a shower.

What the hell, I think. I can do it myself. I mean, a man has to do what a man has to do, right? I roll around the room, gathering up towel, clean T-shirt and sweatpants, bar of soap. I pile all of that stuff on my lap and roll off down the hall to the shower room. At the door, I have my first problem: the door isn't automatic. I mean, you have to pull it open. This is okay when a nurse like Edward is in charge; he just throws your chair into reverse, reaches behind to open the door and hauls you in backward. Easy as pie.

Now it's like some bizarre trick problem in physics. A high school course I passed with a spectacular and hard-fought D, I must report, due entirely to the tutor I had in the NYC hospital. Luckily, the hall is quiet, people settled down, supper long over, most visitors gone home. From the chair, I can pull on the handle and get the door to open partway, but then I can't roll in. If I stand up and get behind the chair, I can hold on to the handles and push, but can't reach the door handle. It is totally crazy that this is so difficult. I know there's a way. There's got to be a way. So what I decide to do is this: I stand up in front of the chair and get the door partly open. Then I try to pull the chair behind me, wedging it into the doorway. This does not go well. Screw it, I decide. I push the chair out of the doorway, letting the door swing shut behind me. I grab my stuff from the chair, abandon it and begin to shuffle, arms full, toward the door. I have got to say that I now absolutely hate this door. I loathe it to its heavy wooden core. Like this one stupid door is the barrier to losing my virginity and achieving manhood. Like it's some quest thing, a challenge issued by the king in a story, the impossible thing the hero has to do in order to get the fair maiden to fall into his arms. Okay. If I'm the frigging hero, there's got to be a way, and I haven't got all night. Fine. I kind of talk to myself, nice and calm: Just pull the door open, Richard, and step inside. Once in the relative privacy of the shower room, doesn't matter if you have to crawl. Just do it, man.

But it is not easy. I keep dropping something, and bending over makes my head spin, and the little paper-wrapped bar of soap slithers off down the hallway. I'm ready to cry. Some hero.

"Do you need help, Richard?" The voice is right behind me.

I close my eyes and rest against the door frame. It's Br'er Bertrand. Wouldn't you just know it would be him? "No, thanks," I say. "I got it."

The man's hand pokes my arm.

I open my eyes and he's holding the bar of soap. If I let

161

go of the door frame to take hold of it, I'll slip to the floor, I know it. So I just sort of stare at the bar of soap, Ivory, in its little white wrapper. I mean, it's a goddamn bar of Ivory, man, that's all it is. And yet grabbing it is an unachievable goal. I sigh. "Well, actually. If you could just open the door and push the chair inside, that would be great. Just toss the soap on the seat."

He snorts. "Sit down, Richard. In the chair. I will take you and your things in there." He puts his fat fingers on my elbow and holds on while I sit down. Once I'm seated, he piles my clothes and the soap on my lap. He swings the chair around, pulls the door open, holds it propped on his hip and drags me through. He's not, it seems, entirely unfamiliar with wheelchair maneuvers. "Although," he's muttering, "I can't really see why you need a shower at eight o'clock in the evening, anyway."

We're inside the shower room, all white-tiled and smelling like bleach. I wave a hand. "Got a hot date, Br'er."

His pink face gets pinker.

I smile, my sweetest smile. "Not really, man. Really"— I lean forward and speak in a whisper—"I had an accident. Little, um, leakage. You know—shit happens. Got to clean up."

He pulls back and his nostrils twitch, like he really can smell leakage. "Surely one of the nurses—"

162

"They're so busy. I don't want to bother them. You understand—independence is important to adolescents. I'm sure you've read that in one of your counseling books, right?"

He grits his teeth and his orange hair seems to straighten up. "Fine. Let's give the nurses a break. I'll be glad to help." He lifts the clean clothes and towel from my lap and puts them on a plastic chair. He takes the soap, unwraps it, and steps into the big shower stall and turns on the water. "Now, shall I help you get out of those clothes?"

His face is now as red as a cherry. I cannot, I just cannot stand the thought of that man's hot dog fingers on my skin. "Nah," I say. I pull off my T-shirt. "I mean, think about it, bro. You guys"—I wave at his dog collar—"you got a bit of trouble going on, as I understand it, with, you know, boys." I leer at him and wink. "Best for your reputation if you aren't found in here, you know, rubbing soap on a seventeen-year-old." I start to pull down my sweatpants. "Whew, it is getting steamy in here, isn't it?"

The color runs out of his face and it looks all sweaty. Or maybe it really is the steam. He says, "I have other patients to minister to, Richard. There's a call button if you need help." And he books on out the door.

And I'm laughing so hard that, somehow, I get a burst of energy and I manage to stand in the shower, leaning on the wall, with no problems. I lather up my own parts, just like I described to him, and when I'm doing that I think of Sylvie and I have to rinse off quick so I don't blow my wad too soon. And when I'm drying off, I get really, really nervous and shaky and have to sit on a chair to pull on my clean clothes. And then I got to face that fucking door again, but this time it should be easier because it opens out. So I'm hanging on to the wheelchair handles and backing up, pushing the door open with my butt, when it swings open so fast that I nearly fall backward. And end up butt to butt with Jeannette, who is steering another wheelchair into the doorway. And in that chair, like a little princess, is Sylvie, with her clothes and bar of soap and shampoo and lotion and all sorts of girly stuff piled on her lap.

And there's one of those interesting awkward moments—I once heard one of my tutors call them "fraught" —when Sylvie and I shuffle around and sort ourselves out and don't make eye contact.

Jeannette rolls her eyes, gives me a fast once-over look and says, "Fancy meeting you here, young Richard." She squints at both Sylvie and me. "Why are you two both so into cleanliness this evening?"

And Sylvie, of course, recovers before me and she smiles like the sweetest angel on earth. "Because it's next to godliness, of course."

Jeannette humphs and shakes her head. "I know nothing about nothing, that's what. I just work here. Come on, girl."

"Guess what, Richie?" Sylvie says, as Jeannette is pulling her through the door. "It's the cutest thing. Your grandma and my dad went out together. Like, they were best friends. So cute!"

I hear Jeannette grunt. "Yeah, adorable." Then the door swings shut behind them. I swing myself into my chair and roll myself back into my room. I brush my teeth over the sink and rinse my mouth from the little mini-bottle of Listerine that's sitting there. And I'm pretty proud of myself, actually. I did it. I'm clean—in fact, I smell like a two-year-old, all Ivory fresh. I'm ready.

And then I sit there, for, like, ever, not knowing when I'm supposed to go to Sylvie's room and getting more and more scared. Finally, the phone rings and I grab it.

"Hey, sweetie," my mom says. "You putting up with Grandma okay?"

I swallow hard. "Hey," I say. "You sound a little better, Mom. And yeah, Grandma's been great."

Her voice is just a bit skeptical. "I'm sure she is. So, what are you doing this evening?"

I think about everything I could tell her. But, really, there's nothing I can tell her, right? I mean, nothing a mother needs to know. And I keep thinking that Sylvie's calling, trying to reach me and getting pissed that she can't and that she's getting ready to call the whole thing off. So I'm having a hard time making conversation here. "Nada. Same old, same old."

"Huh. What's Grandma doing?"

"Same. Nada. Sitting around. Watching TV. Playing cards." My eye starts twitching, like it always does—always has—when I lie to my mom. Remain calm, I tell myself, she can't see you, Richard. You're doing fine.

There's a silence long enough to make me suspect that by some telepathic mother sense, she can see my jumping eye. Then she says, "Right. Can I talk to my mother, Richard? Put her on, okay?"

"Um. She's not here. She went downstairs to get me a root beer. And some ice cream. We're going to make floats. I've decided to eat a little bit again." Maybe that will distract her. It better, because my eyelid is about to go into permanent spasm.

Another silence. "Really? You're eating? Oh, sweetie. That's great."

Her voice is so happy that I feel like the worst human being on earth. But then I realize that that is the absolute truth and I babble on. "Yeah. Started to get a little hungry and thought, what the hey, let's gas up the old engine."

That sounds so stupid that now I feel like the dumbest human being on earth.

"Hungry? You're actually hungry? Oh, Richie, that's wonderful."

She's, like, starting to cry, she's so pleased. Before I have to fall to my knees and confess everything, I say, "Listen, Ma, I'll have Grandma call when she gets back. Okay?"

"Sure, okay. I love you, baby."

"Love you, too." I go to put down the phone and it slides out of my hand, my palm is so sweaty. It falls off the bed to the floor and I have to fish it up, holding on to the cord. Good thing hospital phones aren't cordless or I'd be crawling under my bed on my belly like the reptile I am. Two seconds after I get the thing back in its cradle, the phone rings again. I'm afraid to pick it up, but I have to.

"Have I been jilted?" Sylvie says. "Has that little Hudson High ho called and made you a better offer?"

"No, no. I just—"

She laughs, a wicked little laugh. "Just get your ass over here, Richard. And I mean now."

***

And so it happens. Before my eighteenth birthday, even, I, Richard Casey, become a man. And I'll tell you this right now—I'm not giving details. Not the physical stuff, anyway. This is not some locker room conquest story. This is a *love* story.

And I will swear on every star in the sky and every fish in the river that this was the sweetest event of my life.

A few highlights: Sylvie's room is dark, except for the big old moon outside her window and—how she got hold of these, I don't know—two little candles lit on her bed table. As soon as I roll into the room, I smell nothing but sweetness, like roses and honeysuckle and stuff, in the air and on her skin. I shut her door behind me and push my wheelchair up against it, closest thing to a lock in the whole place. And, for once, I have no trouble walking. Like my feet have wings. (I realize that this part gets sappy—deal with it.) I pull the curtains shut around the bed and we're inside our own little cave. And I have no trouble whatsoever slipping off my clothes and climbing into Sylvie's bed.

She holds out her arms and says, "The hero cometh," and pulls me in. I feel little damp patches all over her sheets, clinging to the skin of my thighs and arms. She laughs and flutters more of them from her hands onto my back. "Rose petals," she says. "I plucked them from that bouquet my friend sent." She takes my face in both of her palms and looks into my eyes. "Our bower, Richard." She pulls my head down and kisses me.

She's naked and everything is—well, I said I wouldn't say and I won't. Only at the last minute, when I'm throbbing and dying to push inside her and she's ready—all open and soft—I get worried. "I don't want to hurt you," I whisper.

She shakes her head. "Oh, come on, Richard," she says. "What are you worried about? Think you should wear a condom, so we don't get some horrible disease?"

And that makes me laugh and then she starts, and laughing makes it all easier, and when she wraps both legs around my hips and pulls me in, I forget about hurting and being sick and everything else except for the heat and softness of her around me. She gives one gasp—more surprise than pain, I'm pretty sure—and then she just keeps time with my breathing. Like we are one creature, pure and simple.

＊

Afterward, I open the curtains a bit so that I can watch the candles flickering and the moon climbing higher until it's above the window and out of sight. I listen to the wind, crying away out there in the world, and for once, I am so damn glad to be in here, instead of out there. Sylvie curls up on her side, her head on my chest and one leg slung over my thigh. "Thanks, buddy," she says. And then she falls asleep. I just keep breathing in her lotion and the shampoo she's used on the fluff on her head. Where she is pressed against my thigh, we're sticky, all mixed up. I love that. I just love it. No way am I going to let myself fall asleep, either. I know I have to get out of her room before her dad comes back. I mean, I know that I'm responsible for her now, sort of like forever, I figure. I've got to take care of her, always. But I just keep putting it off—the leaving part. I just keep holding on.

And I guess maybe I do go to sleep, because the next thing that I know, the curtains are all the way open and there's this great big shadow falling across the bed and a real strong smell of bourbon in the air. The candles are out, but there's light coming from the open doorway.

The *open* doorway. I sink under the sheet and the shadow over the bed growls like a wounded bear and then, I don't know exactly, starts to cry. Not like gentle crying—like great big gulps of pain and fury and you-never-want-to-know-what. And then another shadow comes into the room, smelling like Jack Daniel's, wild red hair, and this one wraps its arms around the sobbing man, and my grandma's voice keeps saying, "Shh. Hush, now. It's all right, it's all right."

And when the big shadow goes down on its knees next

to the bed, still sobbing, Grandma says, real soft, "Get out, Richard." And then she's down on her knees, too, and the two adults—the *grown-ups*, man, that's what's so upsetting—they rock and sob together.

And Sylvie whispers in my ear, "Go, Richard. I don't think he even saw you."

And I go. I mean, I am booking. I pull my sweatpants off the floor and I grab my shirt and I plunk my butt into my chair and I roll. The hallways are empty—it's late—and I make it back to my room unseen. I get into bed and lie there, shaking. Sometime, real, real late, Grandma comes back into my room and curls herself up in the chair.

I lean over and say, "Is she all right?"

She kind of sighs and then whispers, her voice all hoarse, "All right? No. He is not all right. But he's asleep. I took him down to that lounge room. He's asleep on the couch."

"No—I don't care about him. Is *she* all right? Sylvie?"

Grandma coughs, a long wet cough. "I guess so. She didn't say anything. She just curled up and pretended to be asleep."

I hate to think of her alone like that. But I guess she's okay. I take the starry night blanket and one of my pillows off my bed and hand them to Grandma. "Here," I say. "Go to sleep now. And, um, thanks."

She pulls the blanket over her shoulders. "I should have my head examined," she mumbles.

*　*　*

The sky is just lightening up when I hear running in the hall and all kinds of voices. I sit up and I know, I just know. See, no one runs in hospice. No one hurries, no one tries to pull anyone back from the brink. No reason to rush, ever. No codes, no resuscitation teams, none of that. Unless, I think, my head all fuzzy and still half asleep, unless it's someone really young and there's still some kind of chance. And there are only two young people here. And it's not me. So it's Sylvie.

I go to climb out of bed and I realize that my sweatpants are stuck to my thighs. I pull them down, and what I see there scares the holy shit out of me. It's not, like, a little sticky. It's bloody. My pants are crusty with dried blood.

I don't know how I even get there, but I'm outside her room when the docs come running. The door to her room is closed, but they fling it open and go in. I see, for that one second, that the room is full of people. Her bed is surrounded, and I can't even see her.

I lean on the wall and stand there, shaking. After a while, the nurse with the white cap, Mrs. Jacobs, she comes out, carrying a bunch of bloody towels. Her face is almost gray. She sees me standing there and her jaw clenches. She drops the pile of towels on the floor and grabs my arm, steering me away from Sylvie's room. She's holding on so hard it hurts.

"What happened?" I ask.

She doesn't stop, but she shakes my arm. "She's hemorrhaging," she says. "Bleeding, Richard. Heavily."

I feel my legs buckle, and even super-nurse can't keep me from sitting down. I just come to rest on the floor and she crouches in front of me, her eyes fierce. Suddenly, she lifts a hand and slaps me across the face, hard. "You stupid, stupid children," she says, her voice hissing. "That girl has almost no platelets. Do you understand? Her blood won't clot. She could bleed to death from a paper cut. You stupid, stupid boy." And then she's got both hands over her eyes and she's crying like a baby and so am I.

But you don't even get a chance to cry around here for more than a second. Because right then there's a kind of roar, like a train coming down the hallway. It's her father. He's stumbling and running. The nurse jumps up and gets in front of Sylvie's door. "No," she says. She puts both hands on his chest and holds him back. "Don't go in there."

You'd think the guy would fight her, would start swinging, would push her out of his way. Bat her away like a fly. But, I don't know, maybe there's something in that

173

nurse's face that scares him so much that he just starts to crumple. That's what I think anyway, watching him from my spot on the floor when I see his shoulders go down and his hands hang loose at his sides—I think that he's going to fall to the ground and never get up. But then he swings around, real slow, in a kind of crouch. And he sees me sitting there. His hands curl up into fists.

The rest is a blur. I ball up out of instinct and cover my head. But that's like covering yourself from a dragon. That's what I actually think when the heat of his breath and spit hits me: dragon. It's all smoke and fiery red eyes and fingers like claws. He pulls my arms down and his fists find my face. I don't lift a finger to stop him. I roll over, even, onto my back, make it easy for him, whatever he wants to do. I deserve it, whatever damage he can do, in the few seconds before nurses and security come running. I deserve every fucking punch that man can throw. I deserve the kick he gets into my ribs. I deserve it all.

Part III

NOVEMBER 4 – 9

14

FOR A LONG WHILE, I float. And sometimes, I fly. My starry-night cape swirls out behind me and there are these little bright flicks of light moving all around in the darkness. I don't know where I am, but I'm not scared. It's warm, there's a soft wind, and a noise, like, I don't know, like a kind of constant gentle humming. The air smells like the flowers on my wall—that lilac smell that fills the air in May. A couple of times, inside the hum, sort of, there's my name: Richie. Richie. I get it that someone's calling me, but I'm too busy to answer. I mean, I'm moving, going forward, heading somewhere. Haven't a clue where, but I'm on my way. Gentlemen, we have liftoff.

* * *

When I wake up, there's a ghost sitting next to my bed. Its face is nothing but white. The light around it is really bright and it hurts my eyes. The ghost is, like, made of light. Painful, sharp, white. I should be surprised, shocked, scared. I'm not. It's exactly what I expect. I mean, it's an honor, in a funny kind of way, right? To be haunted. I squint and look at this spirit-being more closely. In the middle of all that brightness, there are two dark eyes. Rimmed with red, streaming tears. I want to say I'm sorry. That I'm so sorry. But I fall back into sleep before I can get out the words.

✳✳✳

The next time I wake up, the ghost has turned into my mom, wearing a white mask over her mouth and nose. She's got a yellow cotton sterile gown over her clothes. She smells like sheets off the clothesline, just like she used to. And I'm not surprised about that, either. "Hey, Ma," I say. My voice is so rough and low that I'm not sure she can even hear me. She's holding my hand, and I give a little squeeze. "I'm sorry," I say.

She starts to cry for real. "Oh, sweetie, it's not your fault." She pushes the mask down around her chin to blow her nose and wipe her cheeks. Then she pulls it back up. "Well, not entirely your fault."

That's my mom, all over. She doesn't excuse me. Never has, never will. She just loves me. I keep clinging to her hand. "Sylvie?" I say.

She leans over and speaks really clear and loud, as if I've gone deaf. "Richard, Sylvia is stable. She's unconscious, but stable. They stopped the bleeding. Do you hear me?"

I do, I hear her. I try to smile, but my face won't move. I put up a hand and feel the bandages there. Like the Mummy, I think. Good. No one can see my face. Good.

* * *

Third time, I wake up scared, dragon dreams fuming in my head. "Sylvie's father?" I croak out.

Mom leans in again and says, in that same weird, really clear voice, "Security took him out yesterday and he's banned from the floor. Don't be frightened."

My head is all swimmy. "Yesterday? What's today?"

"Today is November fifth," my mother says. "You slept one whole day, sweetie." The white mask over her mouth puffs out every time she talks. It must be driving her nuts.

I think about all of that. "They'll let him come back," I say. "Sylvie might want him, might ask for him. When she wakes up. He's her father."

"Hush, baby," Mom says. "He may be allowed back tomorrow, but only under escort. They're working it out. It's not your problem." She brushes her hand over my forehead, like she used to when I had hair, smoothing, soothing. "Anyway, there's a cop stationed outside your door."

Now that is interesting enough to wake a guy up even more. "A cop? Wow." I go to sit up but can't. My ribs are all wrapped up and, now that I notice, they hurt like hell. And there's an IV in my arm. That's interesting, too—usually there are no needles, no tubes, no anything in hospice. I wave my arm. "And what's up with this?"

She pats me. "Just until you woke up. So you wouldn't get dehydrated. And to give you extra morphine. I got us the cop. I insisted. That man is a maniac. I just insisted. That's all."

I sink back down. "Grandma must love all of this drama."

Mom's snort almost dislodges the mask completely. "Your grandmother has been banned, too, Richard. Now just rest. Stop worrying. We've got it covered. It's not your problem. Hush, now."

I shut up. What else can I say? They've called in the cavalry. The adults are back in charge. But they're wrong, all of them. It *is* my problem. It's a Richard-created, Richard-mess of a problem. And right in the middle of it: Sylvie. I've still got just a touch of her rose smell on my skin. I've been inside her. She's mine.

***

Next time I surface I really am conscious. I know where I am, what day—well, night, now—it is and everything. I can feel that I'm back. My head's clear. I look over to tell Mom that I want something to drink, but it's not her sitting there. It's Edward, writing in a chart on his lap.

"Hey, man," I say.

He looks up. He's got a couple days' beard scruff on his face, and his eyes are red. "Ah. Richard. Welcome back." He runs a hand over his eyes. "How are you feeling?" He stands up and puts his hand around my wrist, taking my pulse.

"I'm good," I say.

"Ha! You are *so* not good." He drops my hand and writes something in the chart. "In fact, you are the biggest pain-in-the-ass patient I have ever, ever had." His voice gets sort of high-pitched and he's leaning over my bed, right up in my face. "You are also the dumbest person I ever met. How could you not know that that girl was in no shape for—for what you did?"

I try to look him in the face, man-to-man. I'm also trying not to cry, so the man-to-man stuff isn't too effective. "I didn't know, I swear. She was all for it, she wanted me to, she *asked* me to. It was all her idea. Listen, how could I know? I'm sorry. I am so sorry." My voice breaks and tears just come gushing out, soaking into the bandages

181

on my face. "I love her. I wouldn't hurt her for anything. I love her."

Edward's face crumples and he grabs some Kleenex and starts wiping my eyes. "Oh, Richard, I'm sorry. Look at me, yelling at a patient. I'm losing it, completely." He tosses the wet Kleenex into the wastebasket. He backs up and sits back down in the chair. "Listen. This entire place has gone nuts. I've never seen anything like it. I mean, there is a uniformed *cop* outside your door. A cop, in hospice. Everyone on the floor is all, like, crazy. There are lawyers stomping around, charges, counter-charges, lawsuits being threatened. I mean, Richard, your *grandmother* threw some punches."

That stops my snuffling. "Grandma?"

He gives a shuddery kind of laugh. "Oh, yes. Grandma. She went after Sylvia's father, screaming like a banshee. Got in a couple good shots. But, really, you know, we're all responsible. Me, I got caught up in the romance, I have to admit, the whole little lovebirds thing. It was so cute, you and Sylvie acting like, well, like typical pain-in-the-ass kids. We don't get that around here much. But that's no excuse. We're adults. We're nurses. We should have known. We just thought it was, well, harmless, I guess."

I sit up. My ribs hurt, but I can do it. "Right. You

thought, what the hell. They're too feeble, too sick and weak to do anything, really. You were all saying, 'Hey, that Richie, he's so lame, he'll never get it up. And isn't it *cute* the way they're acting? Ah, shucks. Let's be nice to the dying kids. Let's humor them. Take them to Disneyland, like some fucking Make-A-Wish Foundation.' You assholes. You total assholes." My voice is cracking, but I keep going. "I'm surprised that now you're not all saying, 'Well, what the hell. Sylvia's dying anyway. What difference if it's a few days early?' But *Sylvia* doesn't think that. She wants every fucking second of her life. She thinks she's going to get better. She wants to keep on living. She's stronger than any of us. She's, like, I don't know—anything but cute. She's *fierce.*" I can't breathe, can't take another breath.

Edward stands up and holds the chart against his chest. "Yes, she is. You're right. She's in there, right now, fighting. Unconscious, barely breathing. But, you know, when you step inside that room, you can feel her—like there's this force field all around her bed. You're right. That girl is something." He gives a small smile. "You know what? For your first time making love, my man, you sure did find yourself a gem. A girl fit for a king. You stay put, my liege. I'm going to take that IV out and bring you some Coke, okay?"

I feel all the madness go out of me. A gem—he's totally right about that. I got myself a gem. I lie back down. "Okay, thanks. Hey, where's my mom?"

He points down the hall. "We finally convinced her to take a nap, down in the lounge. You know what? She's fierce, too. And then there's your grandma. Whoa, baby. You got yourself some interesting women in your life."

Minute Edward leaves, the cop sticks his head in. I mean, didn't I tell you? There is never two minutes of privacy around here. The guy has a round face and he's kind of chubby in his blue uniform, with a roll around his belt. "Hi, Richard," he says. "Heard you were awake. Just thought I'd introduce myself. Officer Glen Jeffers. At your service." He gives a funny little salute.

"Hey," I say. "Thanks. It makes my mom feel better, knowing you're here."

He waves. "Easy duty. Interesting place." He gestures out into the hall. "I never been in a hospice unit before. Usually they put us in the locked unit, upstairs. You know, to watch the sick bad guys."

"Really? I didn't know there was one of those in this hospital."

"Oh, yeah. Jail unit. Just four rooms, but still. Some of those guys, they're handcuffed to their beds—real bad-asses. Half of them are flat-out making it up, hoping for drugs. But sometimes they're really sick. Really sick and still handcuffed. It gets kind of crazy. This floor, it's much nicer. Calm. And I like that harp music."

I shake my head. "You do? Creeps me out, man."

He looks a little puzzled. "Yeah? I think it's nice—relaxing, you know? And you were almost moved to the locked unit when you first got—uh, you know—hurt. Just for your own safety, of course."

I think about that—that would have been sort of cool. Waking up next to some hardened criminal. Chatting about our badass deeds. "Really?"

"Oh, yeah. But your mom said absolutely not. She's the one got our sergeant to assign shifts here. She's quite a girl, your mom." His face goes all sort of dreamy. "I knew her, way back in high school. Haven't seen her in a while. Oh, sorry, Christine." He backs out of the doorway and Mom herself appears, yawning under her mask. She doesn't even look at the cop, but I see, for one second, the way he's looking at her. Sort of like me looking at Sylvie. And that's interesting, too, don't you think?

All sorts of shit seems to be going on. I mean, this place is jumping. I'm sorry that Sylvie's asleep and missing it. But maybe, I hope, she's not completely. Maybe she can hear, and inside that fuzzy, gorgeous little head, she's laughing her ass off, knowing she started it all.

Next morning, two docs come in and look me over. They unwrap the bandages around my face and cluck their tongues at what they see. I put a couple fingers up and feel the damage—there's a line of stitches under my left eye, and my nose is like a huge swollen softball. I'm sitting up, dangling my feet over the side of the bed, and I can feel that I've lost ground: my legs are like soggy noodles. And my vision is all foggy, and there's this dark hole over to the left. Like a wormhole in space or something—just this empty spot, where every once in a while a stream of green lights goes past. I say nothing about this to the docs. Why bother? What are they going to do anyway? And really, it's sort of cool, my own private light show. They do notice that my left ear isn't hearing much. Except a kind of constant low buzzing, with the occasional louder screech. Sounds are, like, bubbling away over there in what seems like the key of crazy, like the sound track for the worm-hole. I smile at the docs. "Hey, it's cool," I say. "Like an acid trip. I dig it." I make a little peace sign with my hand.

Only one of the docs smiles. He's an older guy and he gets the reference, I presume. The other one, little Asian guy, he just shakes his head. "Richard," he says, "you have a ruptured eardrum on the left side. Not to mention a cracked rib. I don't think that's very cool."

"Whoa." I put a hand over my ear and cup it. I'm sort of shocked, I got to say, that it's really, like, broken. But, again, what the hell? I grin at the guy. "Hey, I can hear the ocean, man."

The older doc laughs. He taps my shoulder. "We're going to leave the bandages off now. Your face will be fine. Oh, and there's going to be a police detective here in a few minutes," he says, "asking if you want to press charges. Up to you, entirely. You up to that? You okay with talking about what happened?"

That one does surprise me. I shake my head, trying to clear away the funny noises and the light show. "No shit. A detective, for real?"

"No shit, son. But if you're not feeling well enough, we'll tell them to leave you alone, come back tomorrow. What do you think?"

I think that I'd like some time to think about it. I mean,

really. This is a lot for a guy to take in, with one good ear and one half-good eye. But they're waiting and, you know, a lifetime of hospital training tells me never to make the docs wait. They are always, always in a hurry, and you got to catch them on the fly. And waiting for tomorrow, around here? That's taking a chance, wouldn't you say? Tomorrow is what we ain't got a lot of, right? "It's cool," I say. "I'll talk to the guy. But I want to be up and dressed and sitting in a chair. I'm not dealing with this wearing this stupid gown." I pluck up the offending garment—this one has little pink roses all over it. Where do they get these things? Got to have strayed from the maternity floor.

He nods. "Good call. I'd burn that thing, if I were you. We'll tell the detective to give you half an hour, okay? And we'll send your mom in to help you get dressed."

I make a face. "Come on, man. Not my mom. Send Edward, okay? Or that nurse with the white cap. Mrs. Jacobs. She's okay, too."

* * *

Mrs. Jacobs does her thing, quick and efficient. And scowling the whole time, so I don't say a word. But then, when she's all done fussing and arranging and whatnot, she runs her hand over my bald head and she leans over and drops a little tiny kiss there. "You are a total pain in the

188

ass, Richard," she says. Then she marches out of the room, back straight as an arrow.

Anyway, I'm washed up and tooth-brushed and wearing my own T-shirt and sweatpants when the detectives— not one, but two, that's how important I am—come in. I'm sitting in my wheelchair and feeling about one-eighth human. The main detective is a woman, tall, gray-haired, but with bright blue eyes. She's not in any kind of uniform, just a plain black skirt and red turtleneck. Her partner is a younger man, dressed in a sport coat and khakis. I'm glad I got dressed. You can't hold your own in a nightgown. Following these two is my mom. She got sort of dressed up, too, I notice. She's wearing what she normally wears to work—skirt, blouse, sweater. And that white mask. But no yellow gown and no gloves. She's making her own rules, too, when it comes to attire. Got to admire that.

Mom sits down on the edge of the bed, and the detectives take two plastic chairs. The tall woman says her name is Detective Richter and the guy's name is Detective Johnson. "Hi," I say. "My name is Not-a-Detective Casey."

Mom sighs. "Richard, please take this seriously."

Detective Richter smiles. "Okay, Richard. We just have a few questions for you. Could you tell us what happened the night of November third?"

I close my eyes for a minute. A whole slew of green

lightships are passing through my vision on the left. *The night of November 3, I want to say, was the best, brightest and most glorious night of my life.* But I can't talk about any of that, can't, like, sully it with words. So I just say, "I don't remember."

She raises one dark eyebrow. "You don't remember what?"

That's a trick question, if I ever heard one. Clever detective. "I don't remember anything. I mean, sure, I remember that afternoon and having some really delicious Jell-O for supper, but after that, nada. Zip."

"You don't remember taking a shower?" She taps her pen on her notebook.

I try to open my eyes real wide. "I took a shower? Really? Let me think." I press my fingers to my forehead: thinking, thinking. "Nope. Sorry."

My mom interrupts. "Richie, don't you remember talking to me? Telling me that you and Grandma were going to make root beer floats? Come on, honey. Try."

I shake my head. "Sorry, Mom. It's all gone. I just remember waking up in my room and you were there, in that mask. That's it." My eye gets a little twitchy, and that makes the green lights bounce.

Detective Johnson speaks up next. He's got this smarmy grin on his face and he's all chummy, like we're best of buddies. "Hey, man. You don't remember being *with* Sylvia that night? Nothing about that?"

For a minute I want to punch the guy, just for that sleazy *with*. My hands actually ball up. I look him right in the eye and say, "Hey, *man*. If I did remember something like that, do you think I'd be asshole enough to talk about it?"

Detective Richter glares at the guy and then at me. "Richard, are you telling us that you remember absolutely nothing about being attacked in the hallway and beaten up?"

It all streams back in for a minute. The heat and smell of the dragon. His red eyes. How much I deserved it. "Nothing," I say. "Head trauma can do that, I understand." I lean forward in my chair and I say, word by slow word, "I do not remember one thing about any attack. And I never will."

Detective Richter stands up. There's a small, sad kind of smile on her face. "Okay. I understand. Got it. Fine. But there were witnesses, you know. A nurse, security people. A whole bunch of people who saw a grown man, a large, healthy adult, beating up a kid. A sick kid. Don't you think that's a terrible thing to do? Don't you think that man—that adult—should be called to account for that action? Made to take responsibility?"

I straighten myself up in the chair. "I think that if we were all made to take responsibility for all the stupid things we've done, Detective, there would be a whole lot of people heading directly to hell. Do not pass Go. Do not collect two hundred dollars. Form a line. Choose partners, hold hands." I hold her gaze until her blue eyes drop. I keep myself upright until both detectives have left my room. But when my mom puts her hand on my shoulder, I collapse. I just sort of fold, wrapping my arms around my aching ribs.

She puts her arms around me and holds on. She leans her head on mine and says, "You know what, sweetie? Sylvie's dad wanted to charge you with rape. Statutory rape! You sure you don't want to press charges? You sure you won't remember?"

For some reason that makes me start to laugh. Rape! I remember Sylvie's rose petals and her nakedness. I sit back up. "Yeah, that's me. Wild man Casey. A threat to every female in hospice. Mrs. Elkins, here I come! Coma Lady, watch out! Shit, they better lock me up right now. Put me in a cell and throw away the key."

She stands up. "Don't be so smart. Luckily, you're only seventeen. If you'd been eighteen, he might have been able to do it. I mean, only one week later and you'd have been eighteen. It's not a joke, Richard."

We both stay quiet after that. Maybe we're both

thinking, one more week. That's a long, long time here. And, you know, I lost one whole day by being knocked out. Come to think of it, I do resent that. That's one thing I can be honestly and truly pissed about. I mean, broken eardrum, screwy vision, who cares? But a whole day, gone? Poof? That is a real tragedy.

* * *

I sleep away the afternoon. Sometime around four P.M., there's this little knock on the side of my door. I open my eyes. Mom's sound asleep in a chair that she's pulled into the corner of the room, completely covered by a white blanket, head and all, snoring. I can't quite see who's in the doorway, things are so blurry. But once I hear her voice, I know it's Kelly-Marie. "Hi, Richie," she whispers. "Can I come in?"

I wave her into the room and put my finger over my lips. "Hey," I say. "We have to be quiet. My mom's asleep."

She's standing there, staring at my face, her hands over her mouth. "Whoa. What happened to you?"

And I have to admit, I'm staring at her, too. Her eyes are a mess of black makeup, and her head is completely bald. Totally shaved. And there's some kind of drawing on it. Not a real tattoo—just, like, a marker drawing or something, all in black. I mean, I'm a thing of beauty compared to her. "Shhh," I say. "Come up here." I curl up my legs and point to the end of the bed.

She climbs up and leans against the bottom rail, sitting with her legs folded, Indian-style. She's wearing ordinary jeans today, but on top, a really low-cut, really bright green sweater. She looks like a busty bald leprechaun.

I shouldn't be so interested in all that cleavage. I mean, I'm in love with Sylvie, right? Really, I am. But there it is, bursting all over the end of my bed, and it's spectacular. Who could not look? No guy that I know of. Not a one.

"What happened?" she whispers.

I think about how much of a hero I could be if I told her I got beat up. And how. And by who. And why. Especially why. What a cool story I could tell: sex and violence, the perfect combo. I think about how, after hearing such a thrilling tale, she might crawl up here and comfort me, wrapping her arms around my wounded face and holding it tenderly to her bosom. Her full, soft, blossoming bosom. If only.

No. I think of Sylvie's tiny breasts in the palms of my hands. Like little birds, nested there. I think about the no-memory story I told the detectives. Once you make up a story, I believe, you have to stick to it. No backing off. I sigh. "Nothing exciting. I fell in the shower or something, someone told me. Don't remember a thing. It's no big deal. What did you do to your head?"

She giggles and runs a hand over her skull. "I shaved. I guess, when I saw your girlfriend—what's her name, Sylvia?—and she looked so, like, classy and all, I thought, whoa, maybe that look will work for me. What do you think?"

I think that for a healthy girl to shave her head to look like a sick girl is one of the stupidest things I've ever heard. So wrong on so many levels. I start to agree with Sylvie's assessment of Kelly-Marie: this girl is not exactly bright. But I don't want to be unkind—don't want to mess up my karma at this stage, right? So I kind of smile at her and I say, "It's cute. What's the drawing?"

She lowers her head so that I can see the top. I can't tell what's there—it's all blurry to me. She giggles again. "It's, like, wings. See? Like, bat wings?"

"Oh, yeah." Bat wings. On her head. Again, you've got to wonder about the IQ inside that head. "Very cool."

She leans forward, and that is worth any half-truth I might tell. "I brought you something," she says. She reaches back into her pockets—and that creates a whole nother wondrous sight, I have to say—and brings out a whole fistful of Tootsie Pops.

And that's all we're doing, I swear, when Mom emerges from her cocoon and stares at us. We're just sitting on my bed, both of us sucking on lollipops. Sucking our little hearts out. And if I have just a bit of a hard-on, watching Kelly-Marie's lips working and her breasts jiggling, what the hell? No harm done.

Mom takes one long look at the two of us and then she says, "Hey, kids. I'm going to take a little walk." And she makes a graceful exit. It's sweet of her to go.

Kelly-Marie finishes her pop, a purple one that turns her lips blue. She wipes her hand across her mouth. "So," she says, "where's your girlfriend today?"

I don't know what to say. But then I think I can use her—no one else tells me anything other than "stable" when I ask about Sylvie, and I know that I sure as hell can't roll myself over there and take a look. So I say, "She's in room 302. Why don't you walk over and see if she wants to join us? Invite her over for a lollipop."

Her mouth goes a bit sulky, but she climbs off the bed. "Okay," she says. "Where's room 302?"

Can't count on this girl to figure out the numbering scheme, can we? "Other side of the hall, going back toward the elevator. Last one on your left. It's pink. Can't miss it."

She goes and I wait. Few minutes later, she comes back, and she's kind of dumbstruck. Like, really, even I can see that her face is all solemn. She doesn't get back on the bed. She just stands there.

My heart starts pounding. "What?" I say. "What's happening over there?"

She looks at me. "Nothing," she says. "She's just asleep, I guess. Lying in bed. Real quiet. But there's this woman in there with her? Her mom, I guess? And she's just sitting there, on the chair, like, crying. Like, really really crying."

I feel like a whole lot of Tootsie Roll is coming back up my throat. I just turn my head away and look out the window. I don't see Kelly-Marie leave, but she must, because she's not there when I finally have the strength to turn around.

I T ' S D A R K A L R E A D Y . M Y mom is standing in the room,
clucking her tongue over Phil's drawings, the ones I hung
up. She's okay, she says, with the one of the woman in the
coma, except for those uncalled-for words on the teeth of
the moon and those creepy little angel/demon things flying around. That one, she says, is sort of sweet, the way it
puts everything in the woman's perspective. And she loves
the two guys who are forever young. But she's not one bit
amused by the porn in the family lounge one. "Immature
jerk," she mutters.

I'm pretty sure she means Phil, not me, so I let that
remark pass.

Then she turns around. Her eyes, over the mask, are
beyond tired, circled in blue. Her skin is almost gray except for two red circles, one on each cheek. I read somewhere in an old book about those kinds of red spots that

people with consumption and other diseases had—way back when, they called those fever spots "hectic." And that's how Mom looks, like she's about to pass out from the weird hectic-ness of our little hospice home. I mean, really, the whole place is, like, fevered at the moment. "Why don't you go home, Ma?" I say. "Sleep in your own bed tonight. Get some real rest. I'll be okay. I've got my cop to keep me company."

She sits on the edge of my bed and shakes her head. "Not after seven P.M., you don't. Well, maybe. We'll have to see. That's something I didn't tell you. There's a big meeting in the lounge at seven—a couple lawyers, Sylvia's parents, me, the supervisor of nursing, hospital administrator, like that. We're supposed to work out a civilized arrangement. Given these—and I quote from the letter I got handed to me—'extraordinary circumstances' of two families with kids in hospice and the 'immense stress' we're all under, we need to come to a 'fair and humane accommodation that serves the needs of all concerned.'" She pats my hand. "And, really, I guess we do. We are all in this together, God help us."

I pull my hand away. This is such bullshit, the things no one tells me around here. Clearly, there's this huge adult conspiracy all around me. They talk about me and they scheme behind my back and then they break this kind of news like it's no big deal. It's so annoying and frustrating, I'm ready to spit. "Yeah, we are *all* in this together, all right, even, I might note, me. You forgot me." I point to my chest and I'm aware that my voice is pretty loud. "Major character here. You can't leave me out. I cannot believe you'd think you guys should have this fucking meeting without me. What are you thinking?"

She breathes out so hard that her mask looks like a sail. Then she sort of sucks it in. Then out again. She's thinking so hard that she doesn't even yell at me for bad language. "I don't know, Richard. I mean, do you really want to see Sylvia's father? Are you okay with being in the same room with that man?"

I shrug. "I have nothing against the guy. Like I told the detectives, far as I know, I fell down in the shower. And I think whoever set up this thing is absolutely right—in these extraordinary circumstances, everyone has to straighten up and fly right. So I want to be there. I'm, like, the man of this family. I have to be there." What I'm thinking, in a confused flurry, is that there has to be a way I can get to see Sylvie. We have to work it out so that I can roll into her room and lean over her bed and talk to her, quiet and private, into her ear, whenever I can. See, I'm sure she can hear. And if she hears me, she'll wake up. I mean, love performs miracles, right? You hear about that all the time.

Oprah's sure of it. I'm sure of it, sort of. Almost. Okay, like 60 percent certain.

I spend the next couple hours trying to steel myself to face the dragon. Girding my loins, like they used to say. Girding my skinny-ass loins.

***

The family lounge is just as dusty and sad as ever, but it's more full of people than I've ever seen it. We're arranged in a funny kind of square, everybody else sitting on the couch and a bunch of folding chairs they brought in for the occasion and me in my wheelchair. They've shoved the TV off into a corner so that the families can face off, O.K. Corral style. Me, Mom, and some lawyer I never met are lined up on one side. Sylvie's mother and father are on the other, sitting on the edge of the couch. In between the families, like referees, some guy in a suit and Mrs. Jacobs, who gives me just the smallest of smiles, are perched on their chairs.

Sylvie's father has his head down so I can't see his face. I kind of wish he'd look up so that he could see my stitches and bruises. Maybe he'll feel better—like he got in a few good licks before they pulled him off me. Too bad he can't see the green lights or hear the kazoos buzzing in my ear. I think he'd be pleased with that kind of internal damage—invisible but enough to drive me crazy.

201

The guy in the suit speaks first. "Thank you all for coming. In my office, we've been calling this the Hatfield and McCoy meeting—our little joke." He gives this little awkward laugh, and when no one else does, he coughs and goes on. "I thought that both families, however, would be represented by attorneys." He looks at Sylvie's parents. "Mr. and Mrs. Calderone? Have you brought your lawyer?"

Sylvie's father's head comes up. He still doesn't look at me. He speaks quietly, perfectly civil and in control. "I am an attorney, Mr. Ellis. We're fine."

The lawyer on our side—some guy my mom found on the Internet apparently, a guy who looks like he graduated from law school five minutes ago and who clearly can't afford a decent suit, judging by the shiny blue pants he's got on—starts babbling, and then everyone is talking at once. I sit back and try to stay focused, but it's impossible. I realize that I can't follow any of this conversation because the buzzing in my head is so loud and the green lights have floated right into the middle of my vision. Front and center, everything is green and everything is jumping around. There are, like, little banners of light skipping around, and it's making me dizzy. I mean, I can tell that there's lots of discussion, back and forth, and everyone is talking in nice, calm, friendly tones. I can hear about one-third of that. But that's not what matters, anyway. People's voices can lie. So I focus in on dragon-man and I listen really hard, and after most everyone else has shut up, I hear him say, "Okay, then, that's the deal. I have offered my profound apologies to the Casey family. Ms. Casey has accepted my apology and, in turn, she has apologized to my family on behalf of her son. We have agreed that, given the kinds of stress we are all suffering, it's all too easy for emotions to run riot, and we have all pledged to work hard at controlling our actions, no matter how we feel. And, most importantly, we have come to an amicable solution: Our family will stay on our side of the hall. Your family, Ms. Casey, will stay on yours. The lounge is neutral territory; however, we will take care not to use it at the same time. Thank you, everyone." People start to stand up and mingle around, like they're thinking about shaking hands, but not quite sure that's appropriate.

I keep staring at Sylvie's dad. It's like, all of a sudden, in the middle of all of this perfectly civilized hubbub, there's no one in the room but him and me. Everyone else fades to little gray shadows, their mouths moving but nothing coming out. I keep my eyes on him. And his eyes swing around to me. And they are, like, burning holes in my skin. I can smell smoke. It's not cigarette smoke—it's something rising off him. I can see it, if I look real close—curls of ashy black are lifting off his suit jacket and circling his head. In the middle of everything, he raises one hand, shapes it into a gun and points it at my heart. His lips pull back around a horrible smile, and he goes, *Bang*. And then everything goes dark. Like my eyes just crapped out, boom. I mean, I'm conscious and all. But not exactly. I hear all sorts of voices, but they're all really far away. I'm pretty sure there's a bullet in my chest, it hurts so bad. Then Mrs. Jacobs is bending over me, giving me sips of cold water and patting my shoulder. "Richard?" she keeps saying. "Richard, are you all right?"

I wave a hand. "I'm okay," I say. "I'm fine."

But no one hears me, and next thing I know I'm in my bed, my mom hovering around, her skin as white as her mask.

The cop, Glen, keeps popping his head in, even though they've canceled his watch and he's off duty. He keeps asking if there's anything he can do to help, and when she thinks I'm asleep, Mom finally lets him come in, and they watch TV together for a while. She even laughs, once or twice, at something he says or something on the tube. I like it that he's here, keeping her company. He's a nice guy, sounds like to me.

Eventually, Glen goes home and it's just me and Mom, and she sits for a long time, holding my hand, real quiet. I mumble at her that I'm okay and say she's got to get some sleep. They've brought in a fold-out cot for her, with pillows and blankets, so she's probably relatively comfortable over in her corner when she gives in and lies down. The hallways get quiet. I'm pretty sure I won't be able to sleep, though. There's this constant thrumming in my head, and my chest feels all hollow. I think I know why that is—it's the place where Sylvie should be, tucked against my chest. It's just too empty and cold.

I look out the window and the sky is completely black, no stars, no moon, no nothin'. Seems about right to me, and I just keep staring into the emptiness, for a long time, wishing like hell there was something I could do. Something I could change.

* * *

Things are supposed to look better in the morning, that's what everyone always says, right? Wrong. They don't. They only look brighter in the sense of lots more green lights flashing around the edges of everything I look at. I can't even drink coffee; it burns my throat and tastes like metal. To please Mom, I take a couple sips of her tea. One good thing—the only good thing—is that Mom is allowed to take off her mask today. Some infectious disease guy told her when she'd been fever-free for forty-eight hours, she could. And somehow, she convinced them she was a perfect 98.6, two full days, although her cheeks still look all hectic to me. Mom has a few tricks of her own, I guess. It's nice to see all of her face, I got to say, and she kisses my forehead about a million times before I make her stop. Then she helps me into my chair and I sit there, making all kinds of stupid plans for getting over to Sylvie's side of the hall. I mean, how crazy is that? Having to scheme to get across the hall? Come on. It's one little hallway, man, not the Sahara.

But Sylvie's as far away as if they carried her off to the other side of the world and locked her in a tower. I think about that for a while; in all the stories, the beautiful maiden is shut up in a tower or her castle is surrounded by giant thornbushes. There's a deep snake-filled moat and three-headed dogs or some such nastiness guarding her. And, lots of the time, she's sound asleep, too, under a spell. But the prince still gets to her, right? The prince dude accomplishes it, every single time. He climbs the tower walls or cuts through the brambles, whatever it takes. No matter what, he gets there. He wakes her up with a kiss and, whammo, they're off to happily-ever-after land. Sometimes, of course, the prince has to fight a dragon or two on his way, too. I mean, that's standard procedure. So, really, what's my problem? I love the girl; she's in danger; I've got to get there and wake her up. Hallways, lawyers, dragons—doesn't matter. It's like algebra, that's all. I just have to figure it out, step by step. I have to focus, that's all.

When Edward comes by to see if I want a shower this morning, I say, "Sure," even though I can hardly stand the idea of hot water on my skin. But here it is: shower = step one. Getting to the shower gets me out into the hall, and even though the shower room is on my family's side of the hall, maybe I can coax Edward to roll by Sylvie's room. Maybe at least peek in, right? Maybe she'll be awake and I can at least wave.

So Edward gets the shower stuff and he rolls me into the hallway and Mom takes off for the cafeteria, figuring I'm well-guarded. The minute she's gone, I say, "C'mon, man. Have a heart. I don't want a shower, I want to see her. One little glimpse, that's all."

Edward keeps steering a straight course for the shower room, so far to our side of the hall that my left elbow is damn near scraping the wall. He leans over and talks into my right ear. At least he's got the one that can hear; the man is a nurse, after all. "No. You have to stop getting other people caught up in your misdeeds, Richard. We can lose our jobs, playing around with you."

"Misdeeds?" The word itself feels weird in my mouth. "Give me a break, man. Me and Sylvie, we're in love. We did what people do when they're in love. That's a *misdeed*?"

He doesn't even slow the wheelchair. He backs into the shower room in one smooth motion. Once we're in there, he sits down on the shower chair himself. His wide ass hangs off the sides, and he looks like a giant crouched on a tricycle, his knees to his ears. He folds his hands and lets them hang down in front of him, knuckles almost touching the floor. "Listen," he says. "I sympathize, I really do. Young love. It's very touching. But I cannot get in any more trouble. Me, Jeannette, all of us—we're under, like, a sacred oath not to let you near Sylvia again. And to keep her father away from you. Our first responsibility, we have been reminded, is the safety of our patients. Not, I have been told, playing matchmaker to a pair of kids. Safety, Richard. That whole medical mantra, remember? *First, do no harm.*"

"Yeah, right," I say. "Tell that one to the chemo guys who poured, like, cyanide and arsenic combined into our veins. Tell it to the guys who radiated our asses until our farts lit up. Come on, everyone knows radiation is deadly, right? Do no harm, shit."

He holds up a hand. "Nevertheless. It's my personal mantra. And there is now, I've been told, a formal agreement between the Hatfields and the McCoys. A line you cannot cross. And that is what I'm going to do, honor the line in the sand. Do not mess with me, young Richard. I can't help you."

208

I wish I could stare him down, but I can't. And to tell the truth, I understand. I can't get these good people in trouble anymore. Whatever I think of to do, I have to do myself. I am, after all, a big boy. Damn near adult. So I just nod. "Okay, got it. But, really, I don't want a shower, either. My skin feels like it will peel right off if water hits it."

He shakes his head. "Fine. Let's just sit here for a while, so they'll think I'm doing my job. Okay?"

"Okay." And that's what we do. It's warm and sort of steamy in there, and Edward scoots the shower stool over to the wall and leans back, closing his eyes. I hunker in my chair, trying to think. But instead, I keep falling asleep, my head flopping to my chest.

***

Rest of the day, I just laze in bed. By late afternoon, even Mom seems to have had enough of sitting next to me; she gets twitchy and restless. She goes for a lot of walks, staying, I'm sure, on the Casey side of the hall. Sometime right around dusk, when she's out there pacing, the phone rings. I pick it up, and have to remember to switch it to my right ear, which feels unnatural. "Richard here," I say and then I smile: it's Phil.

He says, "So, my liege lord, should I kill the fucker for you? Because I can. Because I most certainly will, with my bare hands. Any son of a bitch who would beat on a sick kid—"

I laugh. "Nah. Let him live. He's got enough troubles. I'm a magnanimous despot—I can show mercy."

"Shit. I was looking forward to it. But your wish is my command." He sighs, then his voice brightens up. "Hey, man, look out your window in about three minutes, okay? Hold on." He goes away, then comes back. "Your grandma wants to say hello."

Grandma says, "Sweetie, I want you to know that I did it."

"Did what?" My head is pretty damn swimmy, and I really don't know what she's talking about.

She sounds sort of taken aback that I don't get it, but once she launches into her explanation, I can tell she's excited, her voice rising. "Your father, Richard. I found a lawyer who says it will be a cinch to find the guy and get in touch. And put the screws to his miserable ass. The lawyer says that we might not even need a court case—that the idea that we might sue him for paternity of a boy conceived by one of his students, with him such a hot shot in the school system now, why, that might just be enough for a honking big out-of-court settlement. For your mom, Richard. For, you know . . . later." On that word, her voice stops short.

I think about it. "So it's like blackmail, right?"

She huffs. "No, no. It's perfectly legal, according to this guy I found. And Phil's in on it, too."

"Great. That's a comfort. Phil will probably just show up at the guy's house and steal the silverware before beating the guy to a pulp."

"No, no. We'll do it right, Richard. Wait a minute . . ." Phil comes back on. "I swear, my liege. For you, for Sisco, we'll do this all legal. No funny stuff. Totally legit."

I think again. "Even so. She'll be really, really, really pissed at you. And at Grandma. You realize that."

There's a couple of snorts and then both of them say, "She already is." And then they both laugh, kind of sad-laugh, really. Then Phil goes, "She won't speak to us. Won't let us in to see you. Won't take messages. So, really, what the hell."

I lean back in the bed, contemplating Mom's future— "later." If they can pull this off, she'll have some funds. And maybe a nice guy like Glen the Cop will hang around. It's easy to see he'd like to. That's good, that's all good. Or it might be, if I had one drop of faith that any of it would actually work out. But what's the freaking difference, anyway? Faith or no faith, things are always going to happen to everybody we love, "later." Not a damn thing we can do about it. All we can do is try to nudge things in the right direction, I figure, while we still have time to nudge. Like

211

I got any choice: I realize, a little late, that once I started this ball rolling—talking to Grandma like I did, bringing up the question of who fathered my sorry ass—that there's not a chance in hell that she and Phil wouldn't run with it. Not a chance. Once again, maybe I didn't quite think this through, didn't quite consider consequences. What a crapshoot everything is. All you can do is roll the dice, right? "Sure," I say. "Go for it."

"All right! Now, go on, look out the window. But don't hang up. We got liftoff. Look!"

So I sit in bed, hanging on to the phone and looking out into the darkening sky. In a few seconds, this huge round helium balloon comes up, hanging in front of the window for about three seconds before it blows away. But that's long enough for me to see it: a huge silvery circle with HAPPY BIRTHDAY! in big swirly red letters on it. "Cool," I say into the phone. "Very cool. Thanks, you guys." I don't want to hear what they say about it being a little bit early, and I sure don't want to say good-bye, so I just go, "Oops, gotta go. Docs are here," and I hang up. And I watch as the tail of the balloon, a long long strand of silver ribbon, follows it up and up and up. Up, up and away.

AFTER ALL OF THAT, I'm exhausted. But restless, too. All antsy. Thinking about rolling the dice, nudging fate—that just makes me madder and madder that I can't get to Sylvie. And being mad gives me some energy, so I struggle myself into the wheelchair and I roll just into the doorway and sit there. I keep thinking there will be a few seconds when I can do it. I can roll over there quiet and fast. Supper trays are coming, and it's a busy time. Everyone's got to be distracted for a few seconds sometime. I just have to be patient and watchful. I'll get my chance.

I can't see into Sylvie's room from my doorway. I can only see the rooms straight across the hall: the woman in the coma and the former two old guys, now one old guy. It's so stupid; I mean, it's all of about ten feet wide, that hallway, but it's like the Rubicon or the Red Sea or something.

Or what's the one that runs by hell—the Styx? I feel like if I even attempt a crossing, alarm bells will go off.

But if I roll just a little ways, up to the nurses' station, I might be able to lean over—from my side, of course—and at least get a peek. So I start off on that little jaunt, very careful to stay on my designated side. And right away, I can feel how much I'm slipping. I can barely roll the chair, my arms are so weak. And whenever I lean forward, my chest hurts, right where Sylvie's dad fired that invisible bullet. I have to squint to even see my feet, my eyes are so dim. And when I do sort of get the feet in focus, they're weirdly swollen and puffy inside the clean white socks my mom makes me wear. They're, like, all sausage-like down there. I understand—I've been around hospitals too long not to: add swollen feet to the fact that I hardly ever have to pee anymore and you get what they like to call renal insufficiency. Even we peasants understand that equation: fat feet = kidney failure. And when you get kidney failure—well, let's just say you haven't got a whole lot of time to be a hero. And the whole time you're trying, your mind fogs in and out, too, what with the poisons mounting up in your blood. But, what the hell, not so much worse than moats and boiling oil, right? Nobody said being the prince was easy. I just keep wheeling, slow as molasses. Not sure I'm even moving forward, to tell the truth.

But I guess I am because I'm close enough to the nurses' station to see what happens next: my mom and Sylvie's mom converge. They're both going to ask the nurses for something—the families are always up there, asking for another blanket, a pitcher of ice water, pain meds, whatever. What I see is all a little blurry and tinged with green but clear enough. The two moms are standing on their sides of the big square where the nurses gather—each mother on her side of the hall. But then, like some sort of magnetic force or something gets turned on, they keep going toward each other. Like, some kind of planetary pull. Gravity times ten. My mom and Sylvie's mom, they forget about whatever they needed and they look at each other, you can see the moment when their eyes, like, lock.

It's like watching a ballet. They're like twin dancers, those moms. Mine is tall and blonde; Sylvie's is short and dark. But that doesn't matter at all. They each move around the nurses' station, coming up to the far end of the square. Then each one takes three steps forward and they meet in the middle—I'm sure it's the exact middle—of the hallway. Where the line is, the dividing line. For a second, each mom stays on her side. And it's like everything on the whole floor freezes. Aides stop carrying trays, nurses look up from their report-writing and their hands go still. Visitors are glued to their spots, Br'ers stop scurrying.

215

Everyone watches. There is not a sound, except some quiet harp notes drifting in from the lobby.

Then my mom and Sylvie's mom reach out their arms and take one more step. And they fall into each other, wrapping each other up in the tightest embrace you ever saw, ever. And there is a sound like you never want to hear, ever in your life. Those two moms just start to wail. It splits the air in our hallway, that noise. It rends our air. It is unbearable. And it just won't stop. It's so awful that you'd think that even Somebody Up There would cover his ears in shame.

In the midst of the paralysis that noise creates, I make my break. Not, it turns out, to Sylvie's room, like I planned. I'm not thinking; I'm fleeing.

I don't know how it happens, but I'm in the lobby. The harpy has dropped her hands from her harp, hearing that wail. She's half-standing, her hand over her mouth. When she sees me, she straightens out. Straightens up. She takes command. "Richard," she says. "Let's get you out of here."

The elevator is empty, and we go down fast. I don't think she's talking, but I'm not sure I could hear her even if she was. On the first floor, she pushes me so quickly that we're at the edge of the ER before she stops. We're facing the little ER waiting room, and in there are a whole bunch of people making the same sort of noise that my mom and

Sylvie's mom made. A whole bunch of people hanging on to one another and just howling. The harpy takes a quick left turn, heading in another direction. I can tell that she's not making choices here; she's just heading in any direction that's *away*, away from these places of hideous noise.

I hold up a hand. "Please," I say. "Take me outside, okay? I want to be outside."

She wheels around and pushes my chair out the sliding glass doors, and once they shut behind me, the noise stops. It's cold out and the air hurts my nose, my throat and my chest at first. But I just keep gulping it down—cold, fresh, painful, *outdoor* air. And it feels good on my skin that's always so stretched and dry now. The harpy takes my chair across the parking lot to a little verge of frozen grass that sits uphill of the hospital. She sets the brake, turning the chair so I can look way off, down the hill, toward the river. She takes off the white shawl-thing she's been wearing and wraps it around my shoulders. She says, bending to speak directly into my good ear, "Take all the time you need, Richard. I'll wait." Then she backs away and I'm all alone.

That's what strikes me as so strange: How long since I've been left alone? No one hovering, no one jumping up into my face? A while, that's for sure. I pull the shawl around me and let the wind fill my ears. It covers up the buzzing. I look down the hill at the city of Hudson—a bunch of lights strung in a loose rope down to the river. There's a train leaving the station down there, heading south to the city. It sounds its horn, long and deep. I close my eyes and think about all of those people on that train, off to the city. Maybe they're planning some Christmas shopping—my mom took me once when I was little, and I can still see those decorated windows, with all kinds of moving toys inside them. Me and Mom, we stopped in front of every one and stood there for a long, long time. My favorite window was full of silvery robots, all marching around, filling stockings. A robot Santa sat in a metal chair, constantly sipping from a metal flask. In another one, there wasn't a whole lot of order that I recall; it was just a big heap of crumpled-up wrapping paper and torn-open boxes, each one with a new toy sticking out of the top. A little kid's vision of heaven. But maybe the train passengers are just going to visit someone. Maybe they're going to work. Doesn't matter. It makes me feel happy, thinking of them—just plain old people, living plain old lives. And just beyond the train tracks, the river, doing its own thing, like it's been doing forever. Fish swimming around in the cold water, doing whatever fish do when winter's on its way. That's nice, too.

I lean my head back and open my eyes. I'm looking at the sky, hoping for stars. But it's a heavy-cloud kind of night, I guess, because there's not a one. Sky's black as can be. Even so, if you look up long enough, stars or not, it always feels like you're falling into the sky, right? You know, it's like antigravity or something? I keep my face pointed up, waiting for that to happen, and I feel something cool and wet touch my cheek. I hope I'm not crying. I mean, I don't feel like I am, but maybe I can't even tell anymore. Maybe I'm always crying. But then there's another cold wet kiss, then another. Then a whole swirl of them, and I get it. It's snowing. First snow of the year. I open my eyes as wide as I can, and I open my mouth, too. The little flakes fall faster and faster and, looking up, it's amazing. They're coming toward me, I get that, they're falling. But it feels like I'm lifting, going up toward them. Like I'm the one moving. I hold my arms out in front of me and it's just like flying.

* * *

I don't know how she knows, but just about when I'm so tired and so cold that I come crashing back to earth, the harpy comes back. She grabs on to the handles of my chair and takes me back inside. In the elevator, she brushes the snow off my shoulders and the top of my head. She takes back her shawl and shakes it. The pile of snow that lands on the elevator floor lasts only for a second.

219

In the lobby, the first thing I see is my mom and Sylvie's mom, sitting on the couch, holding hands. They're leaning together, with heads on each other's shoulders, and they're both sound asleep.

In the hallway, the harpy disobeys the agreement. It occurs to me that this is a woman with no patience for rules, and that's cool with me. She just pushes my chair right into Sylvie's room. There's no one in there—no guardians, anyway. What there is is the silent girl on the bed covered with a patchwork quilt.

The harpy rolls me over to the bed and she says, "Take your time, Richard. If her father shows up, I'll take care of it. I will not allow that son-of-a-bitch to bother you." She goes into the doorway, and I see that she's standing there with her arms folded on her chest. Like a sentry. I'm getting to like this woman.

I stay there for a long time and I try to say everything I need to. That's a lot, but I think I get most of it in. It takes a while.

But you don't need to hear it all, and I don't want to go into how I call to Sylvie. How I talk to her and tell her I love her and all of that. Tell her it's snowing outside. Tell her about the train and the people going to the city, describe the store windows, all lit up for Christmas. Tell her what it feels like to fly. It's too, I don't know, personal. And way too damn big for any words I can come up with.

I roll over and kiss her cheek.

It would be nice to say that she woke up, that she opened her eyes and said, "Hey, Rich-Man." That my princely kiss brought her back to life.

But I'm not going to start lying, not now. She didn't move and she didn't speak. That's the truth. But, like Edward said, there's something happening in that room. Like there's a force field around her. Something pulsing and beating, and I know she's in there. Still there. Like she's just biding her time in there. Like she's waiting to rip the spell she's under to shreds. Like she's waiting to be born. And when she is, she's coming out all elbows and knees, kicking and screaming at anybody— anybody—that gets in her way.

When the harpy comes to roll me out of the room, we stop for a second in front of Phil's picture, the one he drew of the grown-up Sylvie, lying on a bed with her baby. The harpy reads the words I couldn't see and Sylvie never showed me. She points to the baby's tiny shirt and says, "Little Richard."

And who am I to say that's impossible?

***

I think I see light in the sky outside my window, but it doesn't do much to wake me up. All day I kind of slide between dreams and whatever real life is—I mean, there's not a whole lot of difference. Either way, there's lots of swirling green light and lots of pure black darkness creeping in from the edges of my vision, like curtains being pulled in. I hear someone say "pneumonia" and I feel my face being wiped with cool cloths. My head gets lifted up and someone drips water into my mouth.

I turn my head away because I've just started this cool dream and I want to stay there, inside it. It's me and Sylvie waiting in line in some big shopping mall, waiting to see Santa. There are big red and green balls hanging down and fake snow piled around our feet. There are a million little kids running around, shouting and laughing. Sylvie and I, we're not little kids, though. We're ourselves, teenagers. Sylvie's hair has grown back—it's not long, but it's gorgeous, all these little dark curls around her face. She's smiling and we're holding hands. We kiss each other every three seconds or so. Long, sweet, laughing kinds of kisses. She tastes like Cherry Coke. I am so into her that I'm not noticing how the line's moving, but all of a sudden, we're there, at the foot of this huge red chair, and Santa is pointing at us. And Santa is that robot one from the store window. He's all metallic and he's got this big steel smile on his face. He goes, "Ho, ho, ho," but to me, his voice is like Darth Vader's—it comes out of that steel-mesh smile and gives me the absolute creeps. I pull on Sylvie's hand and say, "Let's get out of here." But not her—oh, no, she's not scared. I watch as she climbs up on the robot Santa's knee. She sits there, all flirty and pretty, waving at me. She smiles at me and some kind of little robot elf takes her picture—a big flashbulb goes off in my face, and for a minute I can't see anything. But I can hear. Santa-Robot's loud, fake-cheery voice asks Sylvie what she wants for Christmas. I hear her say, "I want to be there, big guy. I want to *be* for Christmas." I can't keep hold of her voice, though. Or her face or anything. The dream floats off and I keep getting pulled back into this hot, dry room.

Faces keep floating into my vision, too: Jeannette, Edward, Kelly-Marie, Br'er Bertrand, Mrs. Jacobs. It must be pretty crowded in here. But it's impossible to tell if they're really there or not. All the faces flit around, coming and going like wobbly balloons. Except for Mom; her face is always there and is always real, even when I'm asleep. Someone keeps saying, "Please, Richard. Try. Try." I want to say, *I'm sorry, but I want you to shut up now. I've tried and tried, and I'm done, okay? So I'm not a hero. Sue me.*

You know, you can think that, though. You can be pretty much ready and all—and Somebody still has a laugh or two planned for you. I mean, really. There might be a couple surprises, even yet.

It's dark out when I wake up: *blam*. Wide awake. My mom always says that all teenagers are creatures of the night, like we're all vampires or whatever. Guess it's true. I'm full of energy, like I could run a marathon. It's pretty quiet in my room now: everyone who's been floating around all day must have gone home. My mom is asleep on her cot. The only face I see is Edward's, and once again I don't think it's his shift. But he's sitting there anyway, snoring in the chair. The curtains in my eyes have been opened; there's lots of green, but no more black.

"Hey," I say, keeping my voice low so that I don't wake Mom. I lean over the side of the bed. "Is this the most boring room in the place or what? Why's everybody asleep? C'mon, man. The night is young."

Edward sits up and looks completely confused. "What?" He looks at me and his eyes get big. "Richard? Hey, man, nice to see you awake." He stands up and puts his hand on my forehead. "Whoa. Still pretty hot, though." He picks up a thermometer.

"Put that away. I'm fine." And it's true. I do feel okay. I mean, relatively. I'm pretty light-headed and, I don't know how to describe this, heavy-chested. But really, not bad. Must be what big-breasted women feel like, it occurs to me, most of the time. Just sort of weighty there in the front.

He puts the thermometer down. "Really? You feel okay?"

"Yep." I sit there for a minute. And then I say, "Hey, Edward, you ever feel like something's going to happen? Like there's something you're supposed to do? Like, something you forgot about, but it's important?"

He just raises his eyebrows. "I guess."

"Well, I got something to do. I'm just not sure yet what it is."

"Uh-huh. Well, anything I can do to help you do this thing?"

I think about that. "I think I better be mobile, you know? I better get into my chair. Got to be ready."

Edward huffs a little about that, but I'm already swinging my legs—my fat, bloated, don't-seem-like-my-own legs—over the edge of the bed. So he *tsks* and *humphs*, but he gets the wheelchair and he lifts me into it. And I mean lifts: I don't have to move a muscle, and just for a minute, I let my head rest on his shoulder. "Thanks, man," I say.

I want to go into the hall. Don't know why. I mean, I know I can't get to Sylvie, and I know that my kiss won't wake her up anyway. But I also know that I've got to be out there, to meet whatever's coming.

And it turns out that what's coming is Sylvie's father. He's pacing the hall, staying to his side, when he spies me and Edward. He stands across the hall and glares at me. Even from here I can smell the smoke and alcohol on him. All around his head, a kind of orange light flickers. I shake my head and rub my eyes, but it doesn't go away, that light. So I guess it's real—dragon breath, held in. Maybe I'm the only one who can see it, but to me, it's clear as day. He's not quite breathing fire, but it's in there, smoldering.

18

SYLVIE'S DAD STARTS TO walk across the hall. He steps on the invisible line and keeps on coming. I feel like Edward's got his teeth bared. He's, like, growling. Like he's the papa bear and I'm his cub. I say, "It's cool, man. No worries."

So Edward doesn't move and he doesn't push me away. He just keeps his hands on the wheelchair, ready.

Sylvie's father stops right in front of my chair. His suit hangs on him like some kind of wrinkled gray skin, way too big. It's got this little pattern of lines, like I never saw before on a suit: I see, all of a sudden, that this skin he's wearing is scaly. Reptile skin, I think. Like this gray thing is the old skin he's shedding; underneath, he is golden, I decide, with black stripes. Like I always pictured the Great Worm Smaug. I shake the green bubbles from my eyes and say, "Good evening, sir."

"Richard," he says. He smiles and bows to me, a little formal bend from the waist. His teeth are stained and his breath stinks. "I heard you were—let us say—rather unwell today. But here you are, looking hale and hearty, I am pleased to see." Edward starts to speak, but Sylvie's dad interrupts. "Would you perhaps like to pass these wee hours with a game of cards, Richard?" He looks at Edward. "In the family lounge, which is, of course, neutral territory? Are you up for a game of chance?"

You bet I am. Chance is all I've got, right? But Edward is arguing: "I'm sorry, Mr. Calderone, but this young man is in no shape for —"

"How about you let the young man speak for himself? How about you shut the fuck up?"

I think that maybe Edward will leap over the wheelchair and strangle Sylvie's father with his bare hands. So I have to intervene. "Hey. There is no call for that," I say. "I am in perfect shape for a game of cards. Let's do it. Let's roll." I start to push on the wheels of my chair. This is nothing but a bluff because I'm way too weak to propel myself, but it pulls Edward out of his paralyzed rage.

He takes a deep, deep breath and says, "Richard, you will not go anywhere with this man."

Sylvie's dad shakes his head. He smiles now, all friendly and reasonable. "I am so sorry," he says. He rubs his eyes.

"The strain, it makes me crazy. Forgive me." He even looks a little bit sorry. Really, the guy is a shape-shifter. "All I'm proposing is a friendly game of poker. With others, of course. Just to pass these long hours." He looks behind me and says, "You, sir. Perhaps you'd join us?"

I turn around and there's Mrs. Elkins's son. He nods. "Absolutely. Yeah, sure."

"Wonderful. I'll go set up a table." Sylvie's dad almost trots down the hall, he's so pleased.

"C'mon, man," I whisper to Edward. "Let me play. I want to beat that man's ass into the ground. I want to trample his face into mush. Please. Give me this one last chance, okay?"

Edward groans. But he, too, wants to see that man beaten into jelly, I know it. So he's going to let this game happen. Really, he has no choice, does he? You going to turn down the last wishes of a dying boy? I don't think so.

***

It's confusing to me how everyone gets there. I mean, by the time I've calmed Edward down and we've arrived at the lounge, it's sort of packed with people, all sitting around a folding table. There's Mrs. Elkins's son and Sylvie's father and, to my complete and utter surprise, the harpy. Her white hair is in a huge cloud of frizz around her face, and she's wearing something that looks like a long white nightgown. She smiles at me. "Hello, Richard," she says. She's shuffling cards and her hands move like lightning.

I just gape at her. "Why are you here so late?"

She shakes her head. "I'm here with my sister. I often stay overnight."

I shake my head. "Your sister?"

Edward leans down and whispers in my ear. "The woman in a coma. Room 306. Didn't you know that? They're *twins*, Richard. Why do you think she sits here all day, playing that music?"

Okay, so my jaw is about to hit the floor. The harpy and the woman in the coma are twins. One dying, one strumming her heart out, every damn day. The mind boggles. I can't say a word. But I try to cover up my abysmal ignorance with words, anyhow. "Cool," I say to the harpy. "Glad to have you. Hey, what about the old guy in 304? You know, we played with him the other night? Let's ask him."

Everyone in the room goes quiet, and they all look at me. "Oh, Richard," says the harpy.

I close my eyes for a minute. The things I don't know. I think I'm so smart. But there's a whole lot here I've been missing. I pull my chair up to the table.

Edward says, "I am not joining this game. I'm just here to watch over Richard."

Sylvie's father grins. "Ah, King Richard has brought his body servant. What's next, a food taster? No matter. Let the games begin."

It's plain old poker, nothing fancy. We don't have chips, so Sylvie's dad has come up with substitutes, stuff he's apparently lifted from the supply room. Piled in front of him, there are little plastic pill cups, small gauze pads and big gauze pads. We all look at him fingering the piles. The harpy lays down the pack of cards and asks, "So, what are these items worth? I mean, what are we playing for here? I like to know the stakes."

Sylvie's dad raises his eyebrows. "Oh, didn't I make that clear? We're playing for days."

We all stare at him.

"Come, people, it's very easy to understand. A pill cup equals one day. Small gauze pad, two days. Large gauze pad, three. Got it?"

Mrs. Elkins's son clears his throat. "Yeah. But. Days of what?"

"Days of life, of course. For our loved ones. Or for ourselves." He stares at me. He's so tired and so wasted away that his face looks just like a skull. A grinning, clacking skull. "For whatever patient on this floor we represent."

The harpy's eyes glitter. "Fine," she says. "You're on."

I think for a minute. One day, two days, three. Multiply

that times however many go into the pot. Times however many times I can win. That's plenty, I think. Plenty of time for the science geeks to do their thing. To come running up this hallway with beakers full of snake-venom magic. To sprint in here with a cure. Listen: I want to *be* for Christmas, too. For my birthday, even. Like everybody else, I want to *be*.

So this is very, very cool. Here's the thing I haven't mentioned: except for that night with the old guy playing gin, I've always been super-lucky at cards. I mean, ever since I was a little kid—a champion. I was beating my mom at Go Fish when I was four, no kidding. Weekly poker nights with my friends in junior high—I won nearly every week. Eventually, they wouldn't play with me anymore. Late-night games with roommates in whatever hospital room I was in—I won. I always win. And we're playing for days. I am psyched. I'm going to win a whole lot of days. No joke.

"Let's play," I say. And the harpy deals, slapping down the cards like she's working in Vegas.

Don't worry, I'm not going to bore anyone with the whole play-by-play thing. I'm not doing some cheesy Texas Hold 'Em broadcast here. It's standard poker and, at first, everyone's winning some and losing some. We're just playing, that's all. Pretty relaxed, to start. That harpy, though, I got to say, she's tough. Can't read a wrinkle on that face;

she is dead, solid serious. I can see that she wants to win her sister more time, big-time, though I can't imagine why. I mean, really, "Long Time Gone." But there's no reasoning with people about this kind of thing, is there? Life is life, until it's not, right?

Mrs. Elkins's son, he's pretty half-assed about it. Yawning and fiddling with his cards. I bet he's ready for his mother to check out—she probably is, too—and he's just messing around here. Makes sense to me.

But Sylvie's dad? He is dead-ass serious and scary as shit. He's not playing cards; he's in a war. His skin gets grayer by the minute, he's got stubble sticking every which way out of his face, he smells like someone pissed Wild Turkey all over him and there's this weird glow around his mouth. Couple of times I catch him staring at me and I shudder. I mean, the man is on fire. I wish I could take an infrared photo of him so everyone else could see the little flames leaping off the man's ears. I can see them, that's for sure. So, what with that and trying to push the green lights out of my sight, trying to focus on the hearts and spades and clubs and diamonds that keep leaping around in my eyes, I'll admit that I get myself into a pretty weirded-out mental state. I start to believe that Sylvie's dad really is the essence of evil, and somehow we're not just playing for days. We're playing for my soul. Not, like, days. Eternity.

And that surely is enough to shake a guy's confidence, whether he's bluffing or not.

By, let's say, five A.M., Mrs. Elkins's son has dropped. He's flat asleep in his chair, head back, snoring like a chain saw. The harpy? She started to curse, last hand, when she drew crap cards, and then she threw her cards onto the table and marched right on out of the room, nightgown sweeping behind her. Edward? He's crashed on the couch, curled up like a baby, sound asleep.

Of course. This is how it was meant to be, all the time. It's down to Richie vs. the Dragon. Screw Hatfield vs. McCoy. This is the real thing. Highest stakes in the world. Dawn's just coming into the sky outside, finally. There are whole heaps of days lying on the table between us, and we're both out of anything to add to the pot. It's the moment. The one where everything is just hanging there, waiting to tilt in one direction or the other. Waiting for just that one tiny nudge.

And I'm looking at the three jacks I'm holding in my hand: three strong young lads. All mine. Sweet. And he's looking at?—who knows? Well, really, he's looking at me, that's what. He's waiting for it—the blow to fall and wipe him out. He hasn't got a thing, I know it. I can tell. Here's a little trick I'll pass on: it's not the eyes, like some people say, that give away the bluff. It's the lips. Lips tremble, you know? When you really, really, absolutely, positively, no shit *have to win*, lips betray you every time. And Sylvie's dad, his mouth looks like a pair of bat's wings, all fluttery.

I look hard at the pot. I figure there's four, five weeks of life there. Maybe more. More than enough time for the scientist-dudes to come through, right? More than enough for all kinds of stuff to happen.

And I've got the winning hand, no question. I'm just about to lay it down and claim my days—*my* days—when the man pulls the nastiest trick I've ever seen. First, he lays down his hand, faceup. He's got a pair of queens. Clubs and spades. Both dark-haired, dark-eyed ladies—beautiful, both of them. Then he leans across the table and looks right into my eyes. Real quiet, he says, "She's fifteen, Richard. Fifteen."

In other words, I've already had two more years. Hits me like a slap in the face. I already lived something like seven hundred and thirty more days than Sylvie. I look at my three-of-a-kind: Jack Spade, Jack Diamond and Jack Heart. Two of them are those shifty one-eyed guys, little skinny mustaches, slicked-back hair, look like pimps. Third one, Jack Diamond, he faces me head-on; he's the good guy. Solid. I think about Sylvie's tiny breasts, soft as baby birds in my hands, how she trusted me, let me in.

Took me a while, didn't it, to get it? What we're really playing for here? Hearts and souls. Hearts and souls.

I fold my cards up and put them on the table, all their faces hidden, those three young dudes invisible. Doesn't matter, Sylvie's father is not going to look. Can't stand to look. Doesn't want to know. "You got me, sir," I say. "Congratulations."

Sylvie's father sweeps all the days into his arms. He's laughing like a hyena. Tears running down his face. He grabs the days and he takes off, running down the hallway toward his daughter's room.

I sit back in my chair. For that one minute, grabbing those gauze pads and pill cups, Sylvie's dad looked just like her. She grabs, too. For that one minute, I feel like I could love him, too. I mean, think about it. Isn't that how a father should be? I mean, what wouldn't *you* do, if Sylvie was your child?

***

Next morning, I'm back in my room, tied to the bed with oxygen tubes up my nose. But, even so, I keep my ear open and the floor gossip reaches me. I hear that, overnight, the harpy's sister died. And so did Mrs. Elkins. "Tough night," people are whispering. Tough night. I don't think, really I don't, that there's anything, like, supernatural or spooky about those two checking out. I figure that both of them most likely hurried to do it, get it done, while their watchers were out of the room playing games. People do that, I hear, all the time—wait until they're alone. Makes sense to me. When you're all alone and you finally got some privacy, that's when the strings that fasten you to earth go *snap*, and then you got liftoff. Not sure I'll ever shake off my mom, though. She's, when you come right down to it, she's just as fierce as Sylvie. And that's okay. Actually, I'm fine with her being here now. Glad about it. And it's funny—the harpy is still playing, I can hear her. She's still there.

And there's other news, too—and it's amazing. Turns out that, overnight, even with all that *snapping* going on around her, Sylvie rallied. Mrs. Jacobs comes in to tell me that Sylvie's awake. Sylvie's sitting up in bed, drinking coffee. That's what she asked for. Not water, not ginger ale—coffee. Hot, black and full of caffeine. Said it was time to wake up. That's my girl.

I know for sure she'll grab that four or five or however many weeks I won her. That girl is crazy-fierce. Hey, she's got dragon's blood running in her veins. She'll grab every one of those days and run with them. She's going to walk on out of here, I know it. She's got things to do.

Me, too. One more thing to do. It's cool, though. I've got role models. I'll wait for my moment, and then I'll do it right.

I mean, no sense waiting for your birthday when you already grew up, right?

Don't worry about me. It's all right. Shit, any way you look at it, me and Sylvie, we're both going to be okay. Swear to God.

And, really, that's all I got to say.

Over and out.

ACKNOWLEDGMENTS

First, profound gratitude to my brother-in-law, Matt Dyksen, who enjoyed the harpist in his hospice unit and who really did, through it all, maintain a cheerful mind. Many thanks to the readers of earlier versions of this book who gave me such helpful suggestions: Bill Patrick, Tobias Seamon, Dan Dyksen, Libby Dyksen, Erika Goldman, and Nalini Jones. I am also grateful to Danielle Ofri, who published the original "SUTHY Syndrome" story in *Bellevue Literary Review* and who has been a wonderful supporter of my work. Thanks to the College of Saint Rose for the gift of a sabbatical leave to work on my writing. And a very special thanks to Gail Hochman and Elise Howard for sharing their enthusiasm, knowledge, and wisdom.

Finally, to the doctors, nurses, and staff who care for sick kids in hospitals and hospices everywhere, unending gratitude and admiration.